HER HEAD A VILLAGE

HER

HEAD

A

VILLAGE

MAKEDA SILVERA

Press Gang Publishers
Vancouver

94 95 96 97 98   5 4 3 2 1

"Canada Sweet, Girl" first appeared in modified form in *Fireweed Feminist Quarterly* (Fall 1987).
"Her Head A Village" first appeared in *Voices: Canadian Writers of African Descent*, edited by Ayanna Black (HarperCollins Publishers, 1992).
"The Girl Who Loved Weddings" first appeared in *The Girl Wants To*, edited by Lynn Crosbie (Coach House Press, 1993).

The Publisher gratefully acknowledges financial assistance from the Canada Council and the Cultural Services Branch, Province of British Columbia.
The Author wishes to express her gratitude to the Ontario Arts Council and to the Minister of Multiculturalism and Citizenship Canada for their generous support during the writing of this book.

Canadian Cataloguing in Publication Data
Silvera, Makeda, 1955–
  Her head a village and other stories
  ISBN 0-88974-056-9
  I. Title.
PS8587.I274H47 1994   C813'.54   C94-910180-X

Edited by Patricia K. Murphy and Stephanie Martin
Copy edited by Robin Van Heck
Cover illustration © 1993 by Stephanie Martin
Author photograph by Stephanie Martin
Cover/book design and typesetting by Val Speidel
Typeset in Spectrum
Printed and bound in Canada by Best Gagné Book Manufacturers Inc.
Printed on acid-free paper

Press Gang Publishers
101–225 East 17th Avenue
Vancouver, British Columbia
Canada   V5V 1A6

For Marts: the one who knows that village.

Erú kì i ba ori kō sā wonú*

*Yorùbá proverb:
"The head is never so terrified that it disappears into the body."

CONTENTS

HER HEAD A VILLAGE

(for Nan)

Her head was a noisy village, one filled with people, active and full of life, with many concerns and opinions. Children, including her own, ran about. Cousins twice removed bickered. A distant aunt, Maddie, decked out in two printed cotton dresses, a patched-up pair of pants and an old fuzzy sweater marched up and down the right side of her forehead. Soon she would have a migraine. On the other side, a pack of idlers lounged around a heated domino game, slapping the pieces hard against her left forehead. Close to her neck sat the gossiping crew, passing around bad news and samples of malicious and scandalous tales. The top of her head was quiet. Come evening this would change, with the arrival of schoolchildren; when the workers left their factories and offices, the pots, banging dishes and televisions blaring would add to the noisy village.

The Black woman writer had been trying all month to write

an essay for presentation at an international forum for Third World women. She was to address the topic "Writing As a Dangerous Profession." This was proving to be more difficult as the weeks passed. She pleaded for quiet, but could silence only the children.

The villagers did not like her style of writing, her focus and the new name she called herself—feminist. They did not like her choice of lovers, her spending too many hours behind her desk or propped up in her bed with paper and pen or book. The workers complained that she should be in the factories and offices with them; the idlers said she didn't spend much time playing with them and the gossiping crew told so many tales that the woman writer had trouble keeping her essay separate from their stories. Some of the villagers kept quiet, going about their business, but they were too few to shut out the noise. Maddie did not often side with the writer, but neither did she poke at her. She listened and sometimes smiled at the various expressions that surfaced on the woman writer's face. Maddie stood six feet tall with a long, stern face and eyes like well-used marbles. The villagers said Maddie was a woman of the spirits, a mystic woman who carried a sharpened pencil behind her ear. She walked about the village all day, sometimes marching loudly, and other times quietly. Some days she was seen talking to herself.

"When I first come to this country, I use to wear one dress at a time. But times too hard, now you don't know if you coming or going, so I wear all my clothes. You can't be too sure of anything but yourself. So I sure of me, and I wear all my clothes on my back. And I talk to meself, for you have to know yourself in this time."

The villagers didn't know what to make of her. Some feared her, others respected her. The gossipers jeered behind her back.

Plugging her ears against spirit-woman Maddie, the Black woman writer sat in the different places she thought would be good to her. She first sat behind her desk, but no words came. It was not so much that there were no words to write down—there were many—but the villagers were talking all at once and in so many tongues that it was hard for her to hold onto their words. Each group wanted her to feature it in the essay.

Early in the morning, after her own children left for school, she tried to write in her bed. It was a large queen-size pine bed with five pillows in a small room on the second floor. The room was a pale green and the ceilings a darker shade of green—her favourite colour. She was comfortable there and had produced many essays and poems from that bed. Its double mattress almost reached the ceiling. She felt at peace under the patchwork blanket. It took her back to her grandparents' wooden house a mile from the sea, in another village, the tropical one where she was born. Easter lilies, powder-puff trees, dandelions and other wild flowers circled the house. She saw a red-billed Streamertail, then a yellow-crowned night heron and a white bellied Caribbean dove. Their familiar voices filled her head: "Quaart, Tlee-oo-ee, cruuuuuuuuuuu," and other short repeated calls.

She wrote only lists of "To do's."

washing
cleaning
cooking
laundry
telephone calls
appointments.

At the edge of the paper birds took flight.

Nothing to do with writing, she thought. On days like these, convinced that she would get no writing done, she left the village and lunched with friends. She did not tell her friends about the village in her head. They would think her crazy, like Maddie. When she was alone, after lunch, scores of questions flooded her head.

What conditions are necessary for one to write?

What role do children play in a writer's creativity?
Is seclusion a necessary ingredient?
Questions she had no answers for.

Sometimes, she holed up in the garden shed at the edge of the backyard. She had cleared out a space and brought in a kerosene heater. The shed faced south. Old dirty windows ran the length of it and the ceiling's cracked blue paint threatened to fall. There she worked on an oversize ill-kept antique desk, a gift from a former lover. She had furnished the space with two chairs, a wooden crate stacked with a dictionary and a few books, a big armchair dragged from the neighbour's garbage, postcards pasted on the walls to remind her of Africa. There were a few things from her village: coconut husks, ackee seeds, photographs of birds, flowers and her grandparents' house near the sea.

One afternoon, however, the villagers discovered the shed and moved in. The idlers set up their gambling table. Gossipmongers sat in a large area and Maddie walked around quietly and read everything written on every piece of paper. Soon they all wanted to read her essay. The idlers made fun of her words. The gossip-mongers said they had known all along what she would write. Offices and factories closed early, as the others hurried into the shed to hear what all the shouting was about.

They were all talking at once, with varying opinions.

"Writing is not a dangerous profession, writing is a luxury!" shouted one of the workers.

"Many of us would like to write but can't. We have to work, find food to support our families. Put that in your essay."

"Look here, read here, something about woman as a lover and the danger of writing about that."

The Black woman writer's head tore in half as the villagers snatched at the paper. She shouted as loud as she could that there was more to the paper than that.

"See for yourselves—here, read it, I am also writing about the economics of writing, problems of women writers who have families." Almost out of breath, she continued, "See, I also wrote about cultural biases."

"Cultural biases," snarled a cold, grating voice. "Why not just plain old racism? What's wrong with that word?" Before she could answer, another villager who was jumping up and down silenced the rest of them. "This woman thing can't go into the paper. It wouldn't look right to talk about that at a Third World conference." They all shouted in agreement.

She felt dizzy. Her ears ached. Her mouth and tongue were heavy. But she would not give in. She tried to block them out by calling up faces of the women she had loved. But she saw only the faces of the villagers and heard only the sounds of their loud chatter.

"No one will write about women lovers. These are not national concerns in Third World countries. These issues are not relevant. These," they shouted, "are white bourgeois concerns!"

Exhausted, the Black woman writer tried again. "All I want to do is to write something about being a Black lesbian in a North American city. One where white racism is cloaked in liberalism and where Black homophobia . . ." They were not listening. They bombarded her with more questions.

"What about the danger of your writing being the definitive word for all Black women? What about the danger of writing in a liberal white bourgeois society and of selling out? Why don't you write about these things?"

She screamed at them to shut up and give her a voice, but they ignored her and talked even louder.

"Make it clear that you, as a Black woman writer, are privileged to be speaking on a panel like this."

"And what about the danger of singular achievement?" asked a worker.

"Woman lover," sniggered another. "What about the danger

of writing about racism? Police harassment? Murders of our villagers?"

Many times during the month the Black woman writer would scream at them to shut up. And when she succeeded in muting their voices she was tired because they refused to speak one at a time.

On days like these the Black woman writer escaped from the garden shed to play songs by her favourite blues singer, drink bottles of warm beer and curl up in her queen-size pine bed. She held onto the faces of her lovers and tried to forget the great difficulty in writing the essay.

The writer spent many days and nights staring at the blank white paper in front of her. The villagers did not ease up. They criticized the blank white paper. It was only a few days before the conference. "You have to start writing," they pressured her. "Who is going to represent us?"

Words swarmed around her head like wasps. There was so much she wanted to say about "Writing As a Dangerous Profession," about dangers to *her* as a Black woman, writer, lesbian. At times she felt that writing the paper was hopeless. Once she broke down and cried in front of the villagers. On this particular day, as the hour grew close, she felt desperate—suicidal, in fact. The villagers had no sympathy for her.

"Suicide? You madder than Maddie!" they jeered. "Give Maddie the paper and let her use her pencil," they heckled.

"I'm not mad," she protested with anger. "Get out of my head. Here"—she threw the blank paper on the ground—"write, write, you all write."

"But you are the writer," they pestered her. They were becoming hostile and vicious. The woman writer felt as if her head would burst.

She thought of Virginia Woolf's *A Room of One's Own*. She wondered if Woolf had had a village in her head.

She took to spending more time in bed with a crate of warm

beer at the side. Her eyes were red from worry, not enough sleep and too much drink. She studied her face in a small hand-mirror, examining the lines on her forehead. They were deep and pronounced, lines she had not earned, even with the raising of children, writing several essays and poetry books, cleaning, cooking and caring for lovers. She gazed at all the books around her and became even more depressed.

Interrupted by the angry voices of the villagers, overwhelmed by the force of their voices, she surrendered her thoughts to them.

"Well, what are you going to write? We have ideas to give you." The Black woman writer knew their ideas. They were not new, but she listened.

"Write about women in houses without electricity."

"Write about the dangers of living in a police state."

"Write about Third World issues."

"Write about . . . about . . . "

"Stick to the real issues that face Black women writers."

"Your sexuality is your personal business. We don't want to hear about it, and the forum doesn't want to know."

They accused her of enjoying the luxury of being a lesbian in a decaying society, of forgetting about their problems.

She tried to negotiate with them. "Listen, all I want is a clear head. I promise to write about your concerns." But they disagreed. "We gave you more than enough time, and you've produced nothing." They insisted that they all write the paper. She was disturbed by their criticism. She would never complete the paper with so many demands. The Black woman writer was full of despair; she wanted to explain to the villagers, once again, that what made writing dangerous for her was who she was— Black/woman/lesbian/mother/worker. . . . But they would not let her continue. In angry, harsh voices they pounded her head. "You want to talk about sexuality as a political issue? Villagers are murdered every time they go out, our young people jailed and thrown out of schools." Without success, she explained that she wanted to talk about all the dangers of writing. "Have you ever heard of, read about lesbians in the Third World? They don't have the luxury of sitting down at an international forum and discussing this issue, so why should you?"

Her head blazed; her tiny, tight braids were like coals on fire. The villagers stayed in her head, shouting and laughing. She tried closing her eyes and massaging her forehead. With her eyes still closed, she eased her body onto the couch. Familiar footsteps sounded at the side of her head. Maddie appeared. "All this shouting and hollering won't solve anything—it will only make us tired and enemies. We all have to live together in this village." Not one villager joked about her two dresses, pants and sweater. Not one villager had anything to say about the pencil stuck in her hair, a pencil she never used. Maddie spoke for a long time, putting the villagers to sleep.

The Black woman writer slept late, dreaming first of her grandparents' village and then of her lovers. Now Maddie's face came. She took Maddie's hand and they set out down the village streets, through the fields of wild flowers, dandelions, Easter lilies. Maddie took the pencil from her head and began to write. With Maddie beside her, she awoke in a bed of wild flowers, refreshed.

HUSH CHILE, HUSH

"Hush chile, hush before I wash yuh mout wid soap." Ma's voice, heavy against my brown ears. "What yuh talking bout? Just hush! Go back to bed. Yuh must be dreaming." Ma would shake her head, a faraway look on her face, then she'd hug me, quick and brisk, and push me away like I was strange or something.

Each night I got into bed and hoped I wouldn't have the dream. Sometimes it wouldn't come for three days straight, then there'd be a string of nights where I'd call for her to come and hold me close and make things right. Sometimes she'd come, but most times she was working the night shift at the nursing home, coming in just as I was getting ready to go to school. Daddy and I would be finished with breakfast and collecting our stuff, me for school and him for the university where he was studying for his degree.

My daddy washed and dressed me on the mornings Ma worked the night shift, right up until the time when I could dress myself. He was gentle when he washed me, taking care to keep the soap from my eyes. He was more patient than Mama. Daddy cooked most of our meals and he let me help him, not like Mama, who would shoo me away. "Chile, go sit, yuh only meking a mess."

Daddy read to me, tucked me into bed, picked me up from school, cooked my favourite foods. Since I was four years old, I remember Daddy doing those things. If I shouted in the night, he'd come running. "The dreams soon go. Just grow up, hear?" Then he'd hug me close and cover me with my blanket.

Ma worked hard. She knew a lot of big medical words and she cared about people. I started washing and massaging her tired feet when I was seven years old. Some evenings when she came home I would have a big plastic basin with warm water waiting for her. She'd soak her feet and I'd scrub them while I listened to stories about the old people at the nursing home. Some of these folks sounded real nice and I was planning to be a nurse when I grew up. Daddy would be across the room, working on his computer.

"Daddy," she would say, because that's what she called him sometimes, "dis place is sure different from Back Home. No respectable person Back Home put dere old in a nursing home." Ma would shake her head. Daddy always agreed.

"But what to do?" Ma would suddenly say. "It's dere country, dere old people." Then she would start to talk about Back Home. To my seven-year-old ears it sounded like Once Upon a Time.

"Back Home," she'd start off, "Back Home, dere'd be neighbours for dem. Dem would have dem children, grandchildren, great-grands, and even some great-great-grands right dere to take care of dem. Here nobody business wid dem, not even dem own flesh and blood." My father agreed, nodding his head, "Families must stick together. I'm glad we're all together. And our family Back Home stick together." Then they would get to talking about Back Home, the place that sounded like a village in an African tale. This talk would warm me like an old woollen sweater on a rainy day.

Back Home fascinated me, this place where everyone knew everyone for Seven Generations. Granny Mam, Ma's mama, still lived Back Home, and Daddy's parents lived the next yard over. Ma promised me that on my summer holidays she would pack me off and send me to Granny Mam to climb trees, swim and jump rope with my cousins.

Summers passed and I never visited Granny Mam. Things kept coming up that Ma said I wouldn't understand. It made me sad because I thought that maybe Back Home I wouldn't have a bad dream coming out of my head.

———————

When I turned eight years old, Ma gave me my first diary. On the card she said that sometimes it's best to write down things and not talk about them to everyone.

July 10, 19—
Dear Diary,

I am glad that Ma gave me you. I can have you all to myself, how wonderful. I had a really cool day.

Mama made me a cake, a few of their friends came over, we played games, played music and we ate. Actually most times we were on the computer playing a new game Daddy gave me. All our friends left and I was so tired I fell asleep on the couch in Daddy's lap. I slept late the next morning.

P.S. You also have a lock on you so I can tell you everything.

July 14, 19—
Dear Diary,

It came back. Ma went back to work. Lucky for me Daddy was

there to wake me out of it. I love my Daddy. I would be even more scared if he wasn't there.

July 20, 19—
Dear Diary,
    Today was a nice day. Daddy finished his studies early and took me to the park. We played on the see-saw and he pushed me on the swing.

July 25, 19—
Dear Diary,
    The dream is coming and coming all the time and I hate it. Ma is mad at me. She says she is getting tired of dese dreams, dey are very embarrassing, what are yuh eating at nights before yuh go to sleep.
    I hate her. Honest, I hate her like I hate the dream. I wish I could just run away to Back Home to see Granny Mam and all my cousins.

August 20, 19—
Dear Diary,
    Sorry for not writing to you. I've been busy doing other stuff, some with Daddy. I have got a library card so that keeps me busy in the library or tucked under my blanket with a book. Nothing new to report today. I'm feeling down, I don't know why.

September
Dear Diary,
    I started school again. It's fun to get back to see my friends. The work looks easy. I like my teacher very much. I told her I am going to be a nurse when I grow up.

September
    Diary, my dreams are coming back and coming back. Some

days at school I fall asleep because after the dream I can't get back to sleep, and my teacher is asking me if I am sick because I am looking so tired.

October
Dear Diary,
I think someone is opening you. Where did they get a key? Maybe I am just imagining.

Diary, I don't know what's going around in my head. Sometimes I get scared with this dream. I don't talk to no one about it no more.

October
Dear Diary,
Last night I screamed in my sleep. Daddy helped me to go back to sleep.

Diary, I want to go Back Home. I hope on my next birthday I'll get to go. I just can't wait to see Granny Mam, all my aunties and cousins and all the other people Back Home. Ma says there is only one store and lots of churches and schools. Daddy says people still bathe in the river, they even wash their clothes there too. I get so happy when I hear that but Ma always comes in with, Chile don't get so starry-eyed, there is work Back Home, going to the river, drawing water and making fires to cook. And people don't have washing machines and those kinds of things.

Mama went on but I wasn't listening. I was seeing the river, I was thinking about making up the fire for the food and the trees and the birds. Probably I wouldn't have the dream Back Home, probably it would be gone.

October
Dear Diary,
The dream is scary and it feels so real I'm tired at mornings and I hurt all over.

November

Diary, the dream is taking me over even in school. I told my teacher and she called Ma and Daddy for a meeting but Daddy was busy with his studies. They think I'm asleep, Diary, but I heard through the walls of my room Ma having a Serious Talk with Daddy. She told him that the school wanted me to see a psychiatrist. Ma said I'm nine years old, too young for that.

December 15, 19—
Dear Diary,

The dreams stopped for a while and I was feeling good and rested and happy at school. My teacher said she was glad to see the changes in me, then it started again and I'm scared.

December 18, 19—
Dear Diary,

It's getting worse. Last night somebody was hurting me.

December 24, 19—
Dear Diary,

You are not my Real Diary and when I finish writing today I am going to hide you because my Ma tore my Real Diary open and she read everything. She was mad because of what I wrote in my Real Diary. I was getting ready to go Back Home and I ran home to tell my Diary about it but my Ma was sitting on my bed waiting for me with my Real Diary in her hand.

"Shame girl," she said, holding my Real Diary up to my face.
"Shame. Better come let me wash dat mouth out wid soap." Ma did wash it out with soap. I screamed but she just kept saying hush chile, hush.
Daddy was away studying and Ma called up Granny Mam and told her everything. I listened in upstairs. Granny Mam said, "De

devil is at work, de devil got into de poor girl head. Put a stop to it before she send sheself to de madhouse. Dat head of hers will get her into plenty trouble. Do you tink is all dat reading?" Granny Mam said, "Find a doctor, a good one dat can cure her. Dey must have plenty of dem dere."

Ma took me to a doctor, a village doctor like Back Home. It was in a place far from our house. Daddy did not come with us. He's studying for his exams. Ma rang the bell and a woman came out and led us to the side door and down to the basement. The doctor told my Ma to wait. He took me to another room with a curtain between me and Ma. The doctor prayed over me and he asked me to undress. He washed me down with bush in a big tub of water. All over my body with his hands, bush, water rubbing my chest, over my legs, between my legs, all the time saying a psalm. He rubbed my chest, again his hands rubbed bush between my legs and he asked me to tell him the dream. He rubbed bush all over. As I told him he pushed harder on the place where the dreams are kept. I screamed, but Ma didn't come. In a loud voice for Ma to hear, he told me it would hurt but it would get better. He said, "Little Miss, if you need to scream, scream it all out."

"She is almost cured," he told Ma, and she reached into her purse to pay him. "Come back in two weeks time," he told her. "Two to three more baths and she will be better." He sold Ma some powder spray to use each night on me before I go to sleep. The label says GO AWAY DREAM, GO AWAY. Ma bought two cans.

Mama told Daddy about it. Daddy said, "Leave de chile alone. Why complicate tings? She'll grow out of it. All dis is nonsense, dragging de child to a village doctor." His voice got louder and he was getting mad. "Leave all of dat to Back Home, why bring it here." He walked away. Ma was standing wringing her hands, about to cry, but the tears didn't come. I wanted to hug her, but I hated her too. But I kissed her goodnight because she was a bag of worry.

I woke up screaming but Daddy was next to me. "Hush baby, hush," he said again and again, just like Ma. But I didn't go back to sleep. I was awake a long time in the dark. The door was open, showing a bit of light like in the dream, so I shut my eyes tight, three times, and opened them three times. But it didn't go away and my daddy was playing with my hair like he did when he used to wash it. I dreamed Ma was beside me, her voice heavy, "Hush yuh mout chile, yuh must be dreaming. I will wash it out wid soap before yuh daddy come home."

CARIBBEAN CHAMELEON

Y̆ard. Xamaica. Jamdown. Jah
Mek Ya. JA. Airport. Gunman, mule, don, cowboy, domestic,
refugee, tourist, migrant, farmworker, musician, political exile,
business exile, economic exile, cultural exile, dreadlocks, locks-
woman, fashion-dread, press-head, extension hair, higgler.
    Leaving the Caribbean for the North Star.
    Tourist with straw baskets, suntan, skin peeling, rum-filled
stomach, tang of jerk pork Boston-style. Lignum vitae carvings,
calabash gourds, a piece of black coral, earrings out of coconut
shell. Not to forget the tonic juices to restore nature—strong-
back, front-end-lifter and put-it-back. A little ganja, lambsbread,
marijuana, senseh, collie weed, healing herbs, mushrooms; you
can get anything, no problem, as long as there are U.S. dollars.
    Dried sorrel, fried sprat, bottles of white rum, mangoes,
gungo peas, coconut cakes, scalled ackee, cerasee bush and single

Bible. Reggae on cassette tapes.

Travellers dressed to kill.

Woman in red frock, red shoes, red extension hair, black skin.

Dreadlocks, Clarke's shoes, red, green and gold tam, smoking on last spliff.

Cowboy in felt cap, dark glasses, nuff cargo round neck to weigh down a plane.

Woman in black polka dot pant suit. Black winter boots high up to knees, drinking one last coconut water.

Tourist drinking one last Red Stripe beer inna sun hot.

Leaving the Caribbean for the North Star.

Back to work, to winter, snow, frostbite.

Theatre, live at the airport. Older woman bawling, young bwoy whining and pulling at woman in red frock. "Ah soon come, ah only going for a week. Yuh bawling like me dead."

"Forward to di Babylon lights," utters dreadlocks in Clarke's shoes.

"Cho, a tru certain tings why ah don't shot you. Yuh a push up life, yuh waan dead? Bumbo claat, watch weh yuh a go," cowboy demand.

"I was in di line before you," answer woman in polka dot pant suit.

"So wah? Yuh want to beat me?" bulldoze cowboy.

"No, but ah only asserting mi rights."

"Cho, gal, a fight yuh want? Mi will box yuh down. Mi a di baddest man around. Step aside."

"Gwan bad man, gwan before di plane lef you."

JA customs officer has eyes deep in passport, behind desk, trying to figure out whether dis is a banana boat passport or what.

"Well praise the Lord for a nice holiday, tomorrow back to work." Woman in black polka dot pant suit talking to herself.

"Ah, a well-spent vacation. Why do they want to leave?" tourist wonders.

Airport personnel hard at work. Bag weigh too much. Too

much clothes, too much food, too much herbs, too much souvenirs. Too much sun packed in suitcase and cardboard boxes. Temper crackle in dis small island. Sufferation pon di land. Tribulation upon tribulation. Some cyaan tek di pressure. Chicken fat, pork fat fi dinner. Badmanism reign, rent a gun, like yuh rent a car. Gunshot a talk, cowboy, dons, police and soldier tek over di streets. Woman have fi tek man fi idiot—learnt survival skills. Man tek woman fi meat—ole meat, young meat, sometimes ranstid.

Destination America. Destination Britain. Destination Europe. Destination Canada. Destination foreign land.

Fasten seat belt. Iron bird tek off. Fly over di Caribbean sea. A site of Cuba, di Cayman Islands. Plane get cold. Goose bump rise. Blanket pull closer to skin.

Approaching the North Star. Atlantic Ocean, flying high over sea. Goodbye May Pen Cemetery, goodbye gunman, murderers step aside, goodbye dead dogs in gully, rapist, womanbeater, police, soldier, cowboy, Northcoast hustler, goodbye.

Fly higher, iron bird. Away. Goodbye.

Goodbye sunshine, warm salty sea, music with di heavy drum and bass. Goodbye mama, baby, little bwoy, goodbye, no tears, a jus' so. Wah fi do?

Woman in polka dot black pant suit. Work tomorrow. Department clerk. Live-in domestic to work under North Star. Praying that in five years, no more kneeling to wash floor, no more scrubbing clothes, replace that with washing machine, vacuum cleaner. Lady in red to seek better life, tell Immigration is holiday. Send for little boy and older woman when life tek. Dreadlocks leaving the sunshine, collie weed, "just for a time, just for a time, Babylon force I," him tell himself. Cowboy cool, cowboy determine, "Foreign land, north light, fi me and you, anyone, land of opportunity, to buy di latest model gun, to slaughter di baddest bwoy."

Goodbye slave wage, stale food, ranstid meat, tear-up clothes, rag man, tun' cornmeal, dry dust.

Music soft, no heavy drum and bass. Missing home already. Complimentary drink sweet, though, another Chivas on the rocks, another Courvoisier, cyaan buy dem a Jamdown. Plane get colder. Drinks warm up body.

Woman in black polka dot pant suit close eyes, shut out her job in di North Star. Walk baby in pram. No matter what weather. Snow high. Shovel it. Walk dog. Feed the baby. Feed the mother. Feed the father. Clean up after. Wash the clothes. Iron some. Fold up the towels and sheets. Vacuum the carpet. Polish the silver. All in the name of a honest day's work.

Plane fly low. North Star light pretty, shining all over di land. Immigration. Line long. Which one to enter. Woman or man. White or Asian. Black or white.

"Where have you been?" "Where have you been?" "How long was your stay?" "Purpose of your visit?" Tourist, white, safe every time, unless foolish to take a little collie weed, a little spliff. Woman in red pass through, safe, can't touch it. Dreadlocks just coming to play music at stage show, no rush to live here, in a Babylon. Safe. Cowboy visiting mother, polite, nice smile, dress good, stamp in book, gwan through, "Three weeks you say?" Safe. Woman in black polka dot pant suit. "Where you been to?" "Jamaica." "Reason?" "Vacation." "Vacation? Family?" "No. I stay in a hotel." "Why a hotel?" "What yuh mean, sir?" "Why a hotel if you were born there?" "Because, sir, I go on a vacation. What yuh saying, sir? Black people can't tek vacation in dem own homeland?" "What items did you bring back?" "Two bottles of rum, sir, di legal amount, fry fish and cerasee bush for tea." Officer slap ink stamp in the passport. Conveyer belt. Round and round. Lady in black polka dot pant suit pick up luggage. Show stamped card. Over there. Same questions. "How long were you out of the country?" "Two weeks." "Purpose?" "Vacation, mam." "Where did you stay?" "Kingston, mam." "Did you stay with family?" "No mam, I visit dem, but I stay in a hotel." Suspicion.

"Hotel?" "Yes mam." "Take off your glasses, please." Officer look lady in black polka dot pant suit up and down. "What date did you leave Canada for Jamaica?" Woman in black polka dot pant suit start breathing hard. "I have me landed papers right here." "Open your suitcase, please." Suitcase get search. Hand luggage search. Handbag search. Sweat running down woman black face. Line long behind her. Officer call for body search. Woman in black polka dot pant suit trembling. Head start itch. Line longer. Black and white in line. Woman in black polka dot pant suit sweating with embarrassment.

North Star cold. But sweat running down her face. Line behind long-long. People tired of waiting. Impatient wid her, not wid di Immigration woman. "What you looking for, mam?" Question to hands searching. Ripping through suitcase. Disorder among di sorrel. Rum. Fruits. Fry fish. Routine, routine. Passenger behind getting vex wid her. Too much waiting. Lady in black polka dot pant suit try to calm nerves. Think bout work. Up at 5 a.m. Feed di baby. Walk di dog. Put out garbage. Cook di breakfast. Clean di house . . . Anyting . . . to take away dis pain. Dis shame. But not even dat can take it away. "What you looking for? WHAT YOU LOOKING FOR?" Woman in black polka dot pant suit gone mad. Something take control of her. Black polka dot woman speaking in tongues. Dis woman gone, gone crazy. Tongue-tie. Tongue knot up. Tongue gone wild. "WHAT YOU LOOKING FOR? Yes, look for IT, you will never find IT. Yes, I carry through drugs all di time. But you will never find it. Where I hide it no Immigration officer can find it. Is dat what yuh want to hear?" Woman in black polka dot pant suit talking loud. Black people, Jamaican people in line behind. Dem close eyes. Look other way. Dem shame. Black polka dot woman nah get no support. Hands with authority. Hands heavy with rage. Tear away at suitcase. Throw up dirty drawers. Trying to find drugs. Only an extra bottle of white rum. Polka dot woman mad like rass. Mad woman tek over. Officer frighten like hell. Don't understand di talking of tongues. Call for

31

a body search in locked room. Black polka dot woman don't wait. Tear off shirt. Tear off jacket. Tear off pants. Polka dot woman reach for bra. For drawers. Officer shout for Royal Canadian Mounted Police to take mad woman away. "TAKE HER AWAY. TAKE HER AWAY." Take this wild savage. Monster. Jungle beast. "AWAY. Arrest her for indecent exposure." Woman in black polka dot pant suit foam at the mouth. Hair standing high. Head-wrap drop off. Eyes vacant. Open wide. Sister. Brother. Cousin. Mother. Aunt. Father. Grandparent. Look the other way.

Jesus Christ. Pure confusion at Pearson International Airport.

The cock crowing once, twice.

CANADA SWEET, GIRL

Last night mi wake up from a bad dream, men dress up in uniforms dragging me through the streets of Toronto to di Strathcona Hotel. I find miself wash up in cold sweat, mi hands trembling, head hurting and mi screaming.

But this morning mi calm down. I lay in bed like a corpse, getting use to duppy life. I lay in bed, staring at di ceiling in my small one-bedroom asking what sin mi commit. What sins my mother or her mother commit? What is it we do that vex God so? But, I don't think bout that too long, 'cause God have him reasons for everything.

Is time for me to get up. I take care not to wake up Mikey who is sleeping beside me. I take a shower. I dress myself. I go to di kitchen to fix breakfast. I fry one egg and cut a big slice of hard dough bread and mek myself some cocoa tea. I sit down to eat the egg only to find that I frighten like hell bout today. I change my mind bout eating. I wake up Mikey and tell him to dress quick. I fix his breakfast. Toast and cereal. I trembling like a piece of fever grass in di wind. I don't want Mikey to see me like dis. He know today is di day that will decide our future. Him have to see me brave. I try to mek mi voice sound light. I move 'round di tiny kitchen washing up di pots and wiping off di gas stove because I don't want him to see dat I fretting. Mikey ready to leave. He button up him shirt and put on him sweater. He kiss me goodbye. I hug him tight. I feel I giving way, so I let him go, too quick, for he already sense that I worried about the outcome of di day. He tell me he love me and run down di hall of our apartment building to stay wid my friend Bev. I shout to him that I will cook dumplings and steam fish for him tonight. I go inside the bedroom and make up the bed. Mama use to always say to me, "Always mek up yuh bed and tidy yuh house, yuh never know who might come by fi visit."

When I pull di blind in di bedroom, I see a police car stop in front of di apartment building. I listen. I wait. Nobody buzz my number.

When I came to dis country, I wanted a new life, opportunity and fun. I look in di mirror and is a different face I see. Look how mi cheek sink in like death. My nice dress that use to fit so well look like I borrow it from someone three times my size. When I remember how nice I look in it at Bev's birthday party, tears just come to mi eyes.

Is 7:30. I have to hurry. Di appointment is for 8:30. I can't be late, that is for sure. I feel so tired, tired like a woman who just come out of labour.

First night I set foot in Canada, nine years ago, I was twenty-six year old. It was the first time I travelling to foreign. I come to Toronto with another girlfriend. Things wasn't too good for us back home. No job. Nothing. Anyway, we young and we want a little adventure. We save up our passage through a *pardner* we join. It was five of us, and every week we each put in a few dollars into a pool, and each week one of us would get the whole sum of di money. Me and Punsie save up we money until we could afford a ticket. When we ready to leave di island, all our friends think we crazy. Everybody say Canada going to send us back. But we brave. We spirited. So we come. We never know a soul here.

We come through Immigration without a problem. They were nice to us. Not too many questions. We just say we come to visit. The first night we stay at di YMCA at College and Yonge Street. That first night we get to know Yonge Street. We couldn't sleep, we excited and want to know all bout Canada. July and it was hot outside, di street crowded with people. Some leaning up against the walls of closed department stores laughing and talking, others in restaurants, and other people walking lazy-like down di street. We meet a guy we know from Jamaica and he introduce us to some more of his friends. That night we went to two West Indian clubs in di area. We get to know about a festival that was about to happen the following week called Caribana, where di West Indian community and other people come out on di street dancing and celebrating wid floats and dress up in costumes. We really feel like Canada sweet and dat we mek the right move. We even find weself boyfriends. We use to laugh and joke to weself and say, "Canada sweet, girl." But in no time our money done and di new friends and boyfriends went with it.

Punsie find a live-in work in no time. It was far out though. So I didn't get to see her often. I wasn't so lucky. I walk for days and days looking for a job. I buy di newspapers and search and search. Sometimes I take di bus to places that had names like Agincourt, Don Mills, Mississauga. One time I even go on a interview close to where Punsie live, a place call Pickering. Same answer everywhere, "No Canadian experience." Then dem put me out of di Y because I owe dem money, so for two nights and days I walk di streets with no place to go. I spend whole nights in a donut shop on Bloor Street West, drinking coffee and waiting out di night.

Luck finally come on my side. One morning I in di same coffee shop, tired from no sleep, I have mi hand on mi forehead. Don't know where to go. Where to sleep. Di girl who serve mi di cup of coffee ask, "What is di matter?" I was so glad to hear a familiar-sounding voice, I tell her everything. When I finish tell her my trouble she say I can stay wid her in her flat. She tell me her name is Bev. She tell me about a West Indian restaurant on Bathurst Street. "Dem looking for a cook and waitress. You can manage dat?" She look like someone I can trust. So I tell her I don't have no papers. She tell me that don't matter. "First of all, you don't need Canadian experience to cook West Indian food, and don't worry bout papers, dem deh people don't concern bout dat, as long as yuh can cook." I smile for the first time in days. She talk to me as if she know what it like to be in my position. That is why I decided to take her house keys, di address of di restaurant and go try my luck.

Di Chinese man take me on immediately. "Sixty dollars a week, plus meals." He tell me dat wid tips from waitressing I will make a lot of money. I cook whole heap that day. Steam fish, ox tail, cow foot, rice and peas, banana and dumpling, mackerel, red peas soup. I wash, I wash. Pots, pans, dishes, glasses, forks, knives, spoons. Everything. At eight in di night he tell me I can go home, but come to work eight next morning and prepare for a long day. I sweep and wash di kitchen floor before I leave. He watching me all this time. I show him di address on di paper and ask him how to get there, for nighttime always play tricks on my direction sense. He say it close, about five-minute walk from Bathurst subway.

Walking to di girl house that evening, I think myself lucky, for to batter bout pon Toronto streets with no place to go no easy. Mama would bawl if she know. I find di place. Is a small apartment building. Di girl live on di third floor. Is a bedroom, a small living room, a kitchen and bathroom. She have a nice bedroom set, chest of drawers, a dresser with a big looking-glass and a double bed. I open di kitchen door. It have a table and three chairs. Electric stove and a fridge and cupboards. Di bathroom don't have a shower. Di taps rusty. Di wallpaper peeling off di walls. It smell old and musty.

The door open. Is Bev come home. I feel a bit like a spy, searching her place. But that pass quickly. She smile and say to me, "Wha 'appen? How your day?" I smile back and tell her I get di work. She ask me about my pay. I tell her. "Blasted tief, but don't take that on, hold on to it. Someting better will come up. Make sure yuh find out your exact hours or dem people will kill you wid work," she advise me. I start to prepare dinner for us, but Bev push me out of di way. "You go sit down. You on your foot all day."

"But you too," I tell her.

"Tomorrow, tonight you are a guest," she insist. Her face halfway between a smile and a little bit of seriousness. She cook a good dinner, green banana, yam, fry chicken, wid carrot juice. Di food remind me of home, and how much I really miss Mama. We eat and talk, late, late into di night. We even tell a little joke or two. Bev tell me about her people in Montego Bay and her little daughter Nisa. I could tell from her voice that she really miss her. She talk bout herself too. "I come here bout three years ago. You lucky, I come in di dead of winter. Never know a soul, di cold was a real shock, never know a place could feel so, but I come to work as a nanny, so di couple was there to meet me at di airport."

She say she work for two years as a nanny and then she get dis job as a waitress in the coffee shop, and before no time she move up to manager. I ask her why she leave her job as a nanny, for it sound like a good profession to me. "Di job was all right," she say. "The people nice, can't say anything bad about dem, but di live-in situation and me don't gree." I nod yes even though I don't quite know what is dis "live-in" situation.

The weather start turn. November already. The grass get dry. The leaves fall off di tree. I don't go to much parties for my pay cheque don't go too far. When my pay cheque can stretch I buy a box of beer and invite Bev's friends and my friend Punsie to a little cook-up. Punsie leave that first job when she find another live-in work at Bathurst and Lawrence. So she a little closer to us.

I pay half of di rent with Bev. I save a little, if is even five dollars. I put it in the bank, every week. I don't waste money. Like Mama use to say, "Yuh never know what can happen to you in life, so yuh must be prepared." And is true. I don't have no health insurance. I can't collect no unemployment insurance, I don't have no landed papers, so I have to prepare myself for di worse, if it come. They divided up my time in the restaurant. Morning, from eight to two, I in di kitchen. After two to around nine o'clock I waitressing. Two of us work in di kitchen. A Bajan girl and me. Sometimes Mrs. Young in there wid us. But mostly she do di cashiering and di waitressing.

Di work good and steady. Six days a week. Hours long. But I make a living. The customers friendly. Mostly West Indians. Sometime di occasional white. Di tips infrequent.

The thing with me and Mr. Young start nine months after I start work there. Is not my fault. I wasn't interested in Mr. Young. One night I work later than my usual hours and he offer to drive me home. I say okay, but him never drive me home. Instead, him drive me to a late-night bar and restaurant joint. I order a scotch and a steak dinner. Why not, he paying. Before you know it di man start tell me how he like me long time—all talk, I figure. He tell me he discuss raising my pay with Mrs. Young. I laugh and say, "Money, money. Money buy everything, eh?" He stare at me and him silent for a while. Trying to figure me out. Then he tell me I fool. He say, "I thought you was a girl who like fun and have spirit." I tell him yes, I have spirit, I love fun, but I'm a poor girl, so I have to ration my fun. I say, "A extra five dollars on my pay cheque can't pay for fun."

"That is what I want to talk about, Millie, ways of making extra money." He squeeze the inside of my hand, holding on to two of my fingers, like he familiar with my body and we have secret together. I tell him it late and I want to go home. He smile and get ready to drive me. "Millie, think about it." Six weeks later it happen. He offer me money to rent a flat. I take it. Bev apartment was getting small. Her boyfriend move in and things get too tight. She help me find a flat on the third floor of a house close by. I share di kitchen and bathroom wid two other girls on di second floor. He pay my rent every week. I save every bit of my pay cheque, except a few dollars to buy food and other little things. He come there almost every night. Sometime I vex di way he come all di time. But he paying di rent. He's my boss. I work hard for my money.

I get pregnant.

Eventually, I tell him mi pregnant. He ask me who is di father. Mi not surprised. Not at all. That's why I wait a long time to tell him. He ask how much to get rid of it. I say, "I never make that my business to find out, this is my flesh and blood and I keeping it." He laugh, but I see that him worried about di decision. I look at him and I feel bitter like gall, but all di same, I force a smile and say, "Don't worry, your name is di last thing I calling."

Mrs. Young see me everyday in di kitchen wid mi pregnant stomach, but she no say a thing to me. She don't ask me how I doing. She don't ask who di father is. Mind you, she not rude to me. She just don't make my belly any business of hers. And that fine with me.

But di big belly don't stop Mr. Young. He come to my room just as often. I pay my doctor fee and my hospital stay. I don't want no trouble with di law. I don't have no papers, so I don't credit. Bev wid me right through. She stay outside in that waiting room until baby Mikey come to life. Punsie come and look for me. She bring flowers and a whole heap of baby clothes she get from di lady she work wid. Good things. Sleepers of every colour and description, some with buttons the shape of animals.

I go back to work when di baby one month old. I get a elderly lady who live on di first floor to look after him. She remind me of Mama. About seventy. A kind face and a big heart. When I work late she look after Mikey without any complaint.

Mikey is six months old. Even though I know di father, I still surprise sometime when I look at him. Mr. Young face all over my pickney.

Di doorbell ring one morning, loud, loud. Everybody in di building still asleep. So I get up to go to look and there is Mrs. Young. When I open di door, she push herself right in, nearly bounce me down. She say, "Come to see the baby, Millie, hear it quite . . ." I never hear a woman in so much hurry. She push her way right pass me up di stairs into my room. I never see a woman look so shock. Her mouth fall wide open like she catching fly. She look so funny, for she not that good-looking to start with.

"So is true. All dis time you going wid me husband and come to work smiling up. Yuh blasted no-good hypocrite!" I burst out laughing. She shouting louder. I shut di room door. I don't want di noise to wake up di whole house. "You worse than a whore. At least the other girls don't get pregnant." I feel like me a suffocate in her words, so me open back di door. She still shouting. Di house wake up. Now I have nothing to keep quiet bout, so I continue laughing. The whole thing too funny. She coming to cuss months after my child born. I say to meself, "Dis woman must be mad, look how I struggle, and save up the little dollars that I work to mind my baby and she cussing." The more she cuss, the harder I laugh. I laugh like Mama, with my head up to heaven and my hands on my hips. I don't think I have the same effect, though. Mama is big and round and I tall and thin.

At last I say, "Enough is enough, Mrs. Young. My baby crying and I want you to leave my room before I have to put you out meself." I push her out of my room and shut di door.

Is six years now since Mikey born. A lot happen since that morning Mrs. Young come to my house. She fire me from di job. Mama dead. I get a letter from cousin Gem. I read the letter over and over. I cyaan believe di news. Mama gone. I can't even go to her funeral. For if I leave Canada, that would be it for me. I can't come back. No papers and di Immigration people, dem get strict. So I stay right here and mourn for Mama. I write cousin Gem a letter. I tell her why I can't come to di funeral. I put in five hundred dollars to help with di funeral.

I move to a new address, di same place as my friend Bev. On di same floor too. A nice one-bedroom I get. I fix it up. I buy new furniture, a bedroom set, three-piece couch, big colour television set, a stereo.

Bev married now and live with her husband and her new baby. Her daughter Nisa live with her now. She sent for her.

Since I leave di restaurant, I do a lot of domestic work. Everywhere I go looking for a job, dem asking me about my papers. So dat mek me decide to do domestic work. I don't do no live-in though. I hear too much about that from Punsie and her friends. Punsie say she and the people dem baby sleep on the same floor and every time that baby wake up, two, three times at night, she have to get up and feed it. If the baby miserable and won't go back to sleep, she have to stay up. She would say, "Yuh tink that mother would get up and come attend to her child? No, for di work horse can do it. 'Cause I sure she hear her baby crying at night. And di husband, he just as bad, for if him coffee and breakfast don't ready by 7 a.m., mi in trouble." She would suck her teeth and ask me in disgust, "Yuh think Canada sweet?"

Her friends had stories close to hers. The story dem don't stop here, but I too tired, and I have my own problems. But one thing for sure, I always work in di day and come home at nighttime to my son and my little room. Even if it late at night. For when he wake up is me him see.

I been here nine years and I still don't got my papers. I'm seeing a lawyer, though, and he looking into some things for me. Few months back I hear some people saying that people who live over three years in Canada without no papers can now go to Immigration and apply for landed. It sound suspect to me so I don't go down. I here too long to get fool. Dis is my home now, any other is only a memory now. Mama dead. I work in dis land, never tief yet, never tek welfare yet.

Di lawyer say my chances look good. "You have a Canadian-born son, a fine boy. You have a healthy savings account." He is right. Since I put foot in Canada, I'm working. I work long and hard. Dis domestic work take a lot out of di body. But mi not unhappy, for I can provide for Mikey. I still work six days a week. Seven in di morning to eight at night. Two different families. I clean. I wash. I cook. Mi walk de dog. I pick up children from school. I bathe and feed babies. I have Sundays wid Mikey. Sometimes we go out wid Bev and her children. Some Sundays Bev give me a break and take Mikey out wid her family for di whole day. They go all over di place. In summer they go to parks for picnics, and Mikey favourite place di zoo. But in winter months, they go and see all the movies what playing. And every now and then, Bev tek them to church.

The two ladies I work for not so bad like the ones Punsie and her friends tell me about. They have their ways sometimes, for is not everyday they wake up on di right side of dem bed. But all in all dem considerate and kind. Dem always ask bout Mikey and how I getting on, and if I have to switch a day from cleaning, it can be done without much fuss. Just last month one of dem give me a nice full-length silver fox coat, with full leather trimming. She got a new coat for her birthday. She di same size as me, and she pass down most of her dresses to me too. Some of dem she wear one time and she decide she don't like it no more. Better she than me though, for she have the money, she have di doctor husband. One thing I can say for sure, is that when I leave for work, and I ride on that subway, nobody can say I do domestic work. Because when I dress in the morning I look like I doing office work. Some Saturday nights I go dancing wid Punsie and some friends. I love to dance. I dance to all kinds of music. But Sunday is di day I like best. That's when I play my reggae music. I sing. I dance. Sometimes I play di same song over and over again.

Is the month of February. And it cold nuh rass outside. The sun shining out hell, though. It mek me remember the first winter I was here and see the sun shining so bright, I run out without coat, and then the cold hit me and send me running back inside. Anyway, dis Sunday, I dancing and singing. Drinking my beer. Feeling nice. Memory of sweet Jamaica flooding over me. Mikey gone to a birthday party wid Bev. I feeling sweet, I enjoying my day off. Feeling happy. Next thing I hear is a knock on di door. I say, "Who is it?" The voice say, "The police. Open up." I open di door and look out on two beefy-face policemen and a police-woman.

My hands start sweating and I feeling hot like is summer. I don't want nothing to do with di police. I got no papers.

They say my stereo too loud and di neighbours complaining. I say, "Thank you, sir, mam, I will turn it down." I get ready to shut di door, but di tallest of di beefy-faced officers put a big foot out to block me from shutting di door. "Are you a landed immi-grant?" "Can we see your passport, ma'am?" "What kind of work do you do?" All these questions coming at me. My hands drip-ping water now, but just di same I say, "What that gots to do

43

with turning down my set, officers?" They don't listen. They just walking into my apartment looking around like they paying my rent.

I say, "Sir, do you have any right to do this in my own house?" Is then the beefy-face woman show me a paper and say I under arrest for illegal entry into di country. I don't read di paper because it don't matter. They got me. The policewoman tell me to get dress. I just stand there looking at dem, until I feel her holding on to my hands and pulling me towards the bedroom. "Get your papers, passport, and any other identification," she say. I ask her where dem taking me. She say to di police station and then to a detention centre. I say where, and she say Strathcona. I say, "What about my boy?" and she say, "We'll get in touch with your friend and get your son to you."

I comb my hair. Put on socks, pants and a thick sweater. I go wid them in the police car. Everybody in di apartment building come out to see me. I shame. But I hold my head high and smile.

I wait for a long time alone in a room. Then dem take me in another room full of policemen and immigration officers. Dem question me over and over. They ask me when I come here. If I ever get in any trouble with the law in Jamaica. Did I know I commit a crime. I say, "No, what crime?" They say, "You're in the country illegally."

Dem leave me alone. Hours and hours pass. Dem offer me coffee and donut. I take it. Dem question me again and again. Dem ask me if I know other illegals. I say no. Dem tell me I lie. Dem tell me I have to spend the night in di station. I ask for a phone call. I call Bev. She already know from di people in di building. She tell me not to worry, she will take care of Mikey and call my lawyer.

Morning come. They take me to Strathcona. My lawyer come. He say to me, "This is an inconvenience, Millie, and I am

sorry to have to bring it up at a time like this when you are dis-
tressed, but I have to discuss money matters first." I tell him I
have $10,000 in my bank account. He is not convinced. I show
him my bank book. I tell him I can sign a couple cheques over to
him. He smile and say he can get me out. He tell me he still
working on my landed. He say he will get me out in a few days as
soon as di cheques go through.

I get a room to myself with a bathroom. I'm lonely and sad. Di
place just like a jail. No privacy. Guards everywhere. In and out
of the room all hours of di night. Visitors have to sign in and out.
Have to leave their purses wid di guards. Mi not very co-operative. I curse every time they come in my room. I insult them. I
use dirty words. Sometimes I throw my skirt right over my face.
That always embarrass them. They go away and don't come back
for a long time.

I stay in that place for two weeks. Then they tell me I'm going
to court the next day. My lawyer call. He say he talk wid di
judge. He say he will tell me more in court.

They make me go over everything. "No, I never been on welfare." "No, I don't have a criminal record in Jamaica." "I come to
Canada in 1976."

"Yes, I have a bank account." "Yes, I have a son, Canadian-
born." "Yes, the two people I work with willing to come in and
testify I am honest and upstanding." The judge say he deporting
me in one week. My lawyer tell him I have a Canadian child,
that I been here for nine years. That I have savings in di bank. Di
judge, like him not listening to my lawyer, he looking me up
and down. He ask me what I do for a living, though he already
know. I say, domestic work. He say, "Two weeks to leave the
country."

My lawyer say he will appeal. He say he's sure he will win.

I go home to Mikey and Bev. I go back to work. I tell my two
ladies about my case. Dem say dey will write letters of recommen-
dations. They say they will hire me full-time if that will help.

I call my lawyer every day. He say he working on my case. "Don't worry," he say. I keep giving him cheques. Three cheques for $500 each.

We go to court again. Di lawyer ask for an appeal, he ask the judge to give me three months. The judge say no, they can't give me all that time. He say, "Report back here in one week's time, at 8:30 a.m." He advise me to start packing. To sell my furniture. My lawyer keep saying that my son is a Canadian citizen. The judge tell him that don't matter. The judge say, "Your son can stay here in Canada. He is a Canadian. He can be put in a foster home and be taken care of."

Outside I tell my lawyer, "I'm scared real bad. I think dem going to send me home. What I going to do with my son? I can't take him back home with me. Where we going to live? Mama dead! Dis is my home now. What mi going to do, sah?" People I don't know looking at me, like mi talking too loud. My lawyer trying to tell me goodbye, as he going into him car. But I hold on to him hand. My voice loud and desperate. "I will do anything. Anything. I will talk to anybody, di newspaper people, TV people, anything, but I cyaan go back home, not like dis, not in dis disgrace. No."

He say he will contact some people higher up. He say he will work late tonight on my case and tomorrow he will talk to di higher-ups.

I write another cheque for $500.

He take it and say to me, "Miss Maxwell, go home and try to rest. You need your strength."

Is quarter past eight. Fifteen minutes before the appointed time. I thank God for bringing me here on time, even though he don't seem to bother with me much these days. Inside di building I wait on di elevator. Di court room open, I sit and wait. All di seats fill up in di room and is mostly Black people. Is now 11 o'clock and I still waiting to hear my name call and for my lawyer to come.

It scary. I feel like running, but I don't know where to. They call out some more names, and di people move forward. All immigration cases. I step outside to make a phone call. No answer at di lawyer office. I phone Bev and Mikey to say I still waiting. I ask if they hear from di lawyer. I try di number again. No answer. I go back to my seat in di court room. My neck tired from turning left and right looking for dat lawyer. I thinking about Mikey, and his future. "What future?" I ask myself.

Time going by, half past two and my stomach singing wid hunger.

"Millie Maxwell, Millie Maxwell, this way, please." I look around for my lawyer. He not around. I brace myself up from my chair.

"Sir," I say, "My lawyer not here yet. He on his way."

It seem he don't hear me.

"Miss Maxwell, I am sorry but your appeal has been denied. You have exactly one day to do your personal business. You are booked on Air Canada, flight 992, to Montego Bay, Jamaica. The rest of the details are in this envelope."

He push the envelope in my hand. It fall on di ground, for my hand too weak to hold on to it.

"But sir," I bawl out, for me lose control of me senses, "I have mi furniture to sell. I have to decide what to do wid me son. I just pay another month rent on my apartment. I have to buy a suitcase. I have money to take out of di bank. I have . . . "

"Good day, Miss Maxwell."

"Next, please, Mr. Charles Fraser?"

"Lord, Jesus Christ, it cyaan just done so. Weh mi lawyer deh? Who speaking for me? Is nine years, I deh here, scrubbing, cleaning, cooking. NINE YEARS."

"Miss Maxwell, please leave the courtroom. You can be charged with contempt of court."

Four hands ease me towards the door, and place me on a

bench outside. Somebody hand me a cup of coffee.

I get up from di bench and walk out of di building. I walk towards College Street. I turn west on College Street to Bathurst. Today is one of di coldest day since winter start. People running in all directions for shelter. Di streets dry and it look like smoke jumping out of di pavement. Mi nose running, and di snot turn to ice on mi face. Me cold, even di fox cyaan keep me warm today. Mi don't even want to run for shelter. Dis coldness cyaan match di numbness in me.

THE GIRL WHO LOVED
WEDDINGS

I'm a girl who loves weddings. I
really do. I've been a bridesmaid too many times to count.
Weddings can be so beautifully perfect. So romantic. Mystical
even. The bride. Face full of hope. I've seen that look on women
who'd lived with men many months or even years before the
wedding. Women who already had children.

And still that look of wonder. That simple-hearted innocence,
if only for those few cherished hours. I just love it. I can't help it.
I don't know what it is. Yes, I do know, weddings just let you forget the ugliness of life.

The groom. Oh Lord, the groom. Protector. Provider. Till death
do us part. Yeah, I can still hear those countless ministers. I love it,
I tell you. I think weddings are one of the greatest theatrical per-
formances on earth. Only the Bible is better scripted. I really mean
it. And the faces of the guests, worth a million, those faces.

The hours tap away and the celebrations come to a close. The wedding stops and the marriage begins. For some, it's a hairpin curve in the road, for others it's just learning the traffic rules.

Many, many years ago, I was asked to be a bridesmaid at my cousin Helena's wedding. It was to be a small occasion and I, the only bridesmaid. Without hesitation, I said yes.

She chose a small Anglican church for the wedding, close to their apartment, in fact right across from the funeral parlour where our grandfather was buried. Okay, he wasn't buried there. You know what I mean. Anyway, my cousin and I were pall bearers at the funeral. You see, we come from a family with more than its share of women. When my cousin first told me about the wedding, I thought she was pregnant and, not to lose face, was getting married.

"Are you pregnant?" I asked her a few days before the ceremony. She threw her quick, nervous laugh in my face and answered back, "Don't be ridiculous. Nothing of the kind. I just don't want to live with him like this any more. Is that okay?" She had known him for three months, two of which they shacked up together.

My cousin was a girl with many curves, a pretty face, long straightened black hair that rested on her shoulders, and a smile so dazzling that it just about pulled you into her mouth. She was also unpredictable. Once, not so long before she announced her wedding plans, she confided in me that she would never ever get married.

"Jenny," she said. "Girl, I know I will definitely not do this married thing, I don't want anyone controlling me. No way. I'm happy the way I am. I love them, but not enough to marry."

Of course, when we were both twelve years old, she'd said she would never have sex with a boy. In fact, if you want to know the truth, we had made that pledge to each other. But, no sooner said, she ran off with Everet Johnson when she was thirteen years old. Needless to say, cousin Helena fell in love several times after Everet Johnson. At fifteen, she wanted to be an actress, ran off to Calgary, then Vancouver and finally Quebec. She worked the bars as a striptease dancer and made some extra money on the side as an occasional small-time call girl.

One day I received an ominous brown package in the mail. It was from her. A full-page profile of Helena in a magazine called *Le Nouveau*. Having never been to Montreal, I was not familiar with this magazine. I did recognize the full-page, colour, nude centrefold, though. There she was, her beautiful self, head high, black hair on brown shoulders and that award-winning smile. Her youthful naked body on view for the small price of a magazine. With my limited French, I set my sights on making sense out of the article.

Cousin Helena had changed her name to Natasha the Stripper. In the interview, she said she was twenty-two years old. I looked into her then sixteen-year-old face, heavy with make-up, and wondered how on earth the interviewer could not see the youth in her. Did they even care, I wondered. Still, I could not help but chuckle at the parts of the interview I could understand. She claimed she had recently come from the Caribbean to Quebec. That cousin of mine. We were both Canadian-born of Caribbean parents, and we had only visited our parents' birthplace once. The more I read, the louder my laughter. She told the interviewer that she could never get used to the harsh Canadian winter, but the Canadian people were gentle and warm, less racist, she said, than the people across the border. What a sweet liar this cousin of mine.

I was at first embarrassed by the nude photo. Legs wide apart, one hand holding dark brown breast, the other bashfully covering her pubic hair. But I had to admit, she did look damn good. I quickly hid the newspaper away from my parents' inquisitive eyes.

When she got tired of Quebec, she ran off to Las Vegas, with a customer from a night club where she had worked. She returned home a year later, with a broken heart and a series of STDs. But soon she was laughing that nervy laugh and chalking it all up to experience.

Some of our friends thought she was crazy. "A loose screw somewhere," they used to say. But we paid no attention to their cruel talk. They're all just envious, I comforted her.

To me, Helena was simply a free spirit. She courted adventure and lived life to its fullest. She was not content to live through books. I'm not saying that sometimes she didn't do crazy things, but it was not a craziness that sends you to the asylum. Goddammit, I would have been right beside her, and I'm not mad.

My cousin just had high spirits. Like the time she drove her father's car all the way to Niagara Falls without a license. I was sitting deep in the back seat with Douglas, my first boyfriend. Everet Johnson was up front with Helena. In fact, it was a sweet ride and we didn't get caught. Does she sound like a candidate for a mental asylum? Oh yes, she did once piss in the middle of a department store to protest the treatment of a young immigrant boy caught shoplifting. Fortunately for us, we were not discovered.

Then there was the time we sneaked out my bedroom window, from the second floor of our house, to attend a dance. We were grounded, so asking permission was strictly out of the question. Desperate to show our faces at that school dance, salvation came to us in the form of an eight-foot ladder which we hid inconspicuously in my bedroom.

I was surprised we did not wake my parents when we came home. Our voices heavy with wine and our balance in question, we climbed into bed, where sleep soon found us, legs flung over legs.

There were many such adventures with cousin Helena. Then I broke the spell. Got married and separated shortly after. Helena continued to blaze ahead. Finally, she met Monty. Fell in Love.

Shacked up. Joined his church. And now they were to be married.

Monty was tall and slim. Quiet. A bit on the serious side. He didn't laugh easily. He was almost thirty years old, ten years older than Helena, eight years my senior. He wasn't ugly, but neither was he handsome. Monty's hair was shoulder length, like Helena's. Unlike Helena's straightened hair, his was in thick brown dreads. His eyes were a dark broody brown, coloured with red specks. He had a wide nose and full lips. His face sported a long, thin cut on the right side, from his ears to the tip of his mouth. A knife wound, I learned later. A souvenir from his former days as a small-time hustler.

Monty was a guy with no trade. When he could, he worked as a packer in a meat market, but he never stayed long enough to get any seniority. Other times, he drove cabs. The evenings I spent over at my cousin Helena's house he was easy enough to be around, though a bit unravelled in his thread of conversation.

He was an orthodox Rastafarian, though he did not attend church regularly. Many times I tried to engage him in discussions about his religion and the teachings of the movement, but to no avail. I was not ignorant of the Rastafarian philosophy and wanted to have a more in-depth discussion with Monty, but we never got past Ethiopia, Haile Selassie, or the cloud of smoke always coming from his nostrils. When I told Helena about his unwillingness to discuss his faith, she told me he was a deep thinker. To me, Monty was a fraud. An incorrigible one. But the more I got to know him, the easier it was for me to understand my cousin's attraction to this man.

Once, furious after yet another demonstration to protest the injustice of the world, I stopped by their apartment. I was particularly agitated that day. My feet were swollen to almost twice their size. My clothes, sticky and smelly from the hot sun and close crowd. The sound of police sirens was still in my ears. My cousin was not in. I was almost in tears as I threw myself onto the couch.

"When will this madness in South Africa end? When will Blacks have basic equal rights? Justice? Determination of their own lives? I'm tired of pounding those damn pavements." If he were a stranger in a crowded room, I would have gotten a better response. He was sitting right there next to me on the couch, nodding in agreement.

"Don't you have anything to say?" I asked, my voice quivering. "Where do you think this is all going to end? What do you think of people taking up arms, fighting violence with violence?" He must have been surprised by the tremor in my voice, for he responded somewhat.

"Well, whatever is necessary, though I is a peaceful man."

"Well, then," I pressed, "what's to be done?"

"Well, Africa must be free no matter what." I looked at him, puzzled and disappointed with his answer. I opened my mouth to proceed, but he wandered off towards the bathroom with a match and a cigarette.

"I'm going to take a shit, help yourself to some food from the stove."

Deep thinker my ass. How could my cousin marry this jerk? At that moment if it weren't for my love for Helena and the chance to be a bridesmaid once again, I would have left that blasted apartment.

He was a long time on the toilet. When he finally emerged, he patted me on my shoulder and spoke like one who had just had a vision. "Don't get so worked up, little sister, leave everything to Jah. South Africa time soon come, and all dem wicked ones will get burn ... "

I was irritated but kept my comments to a heavy sigh.

"Let me play something to calm you down," he offered, walking over to the sound system. Curled up on the couch, I fell into a light sleep, listening to a selection of reggae singers and sniffing an occasional whiff of Monty's spliff. Music and a joint: that was Mr. Deep-Thinking future cousin-in-law's answer to everything.

Despite Monty, I was still excited about the wedding. I myself had married young. Only eighteen years old. My husband ran out on me three months and four days after the ceremony. I know just when he left and why. We had both found out I was barren. But my lack of menstrual blood did not bother me until my husband left me for a woman with a womb as big as a continent. In no time she gave him twins. I felt like hell on wheels. I was tormented by his happy family and ashamed that he'd walked out on me. Our ill-fated marriage was the talk of the town for a long time. I wanted to kill myself and I wanted revenge on him.

Ours had been an old-fashioned Christian wedding. Two hundred guests on each side. I wore my mother's long white wedding gown. I'd even converted to Catholicism for him. In the overcrowded church, I repeated "Till death do us part."

For months after the marriage ended, I imagined ways of killing myself. Dreamed about the look of horror on his face, his guilt. I wasn't thinking feminism back then. I was possessed. I wanted only one thing. My man back. My marriage back. I wanted to marry all over again. I wanted to repeat those vows.

I took an overdose, a mixture of sleeping pills and aspirins, and woke up in the psychiatric ward. I resigned myself to a three-week involuntary stay. Another time, tired of being alone, tired of thinking about him, I rushed from my bed, onto the street, wearing only a cotton long-sleeved shirt that had belonged to him, and plunged into a moving van. I was knocked to the side of the road but was not seriously injured. The driver was not very sensitive and stoned me with obscenities. "Fuckin' bitch, you wanna turn me into a murderer? Fuckin' sleaze, why don't you go blow your brains out?"

In between, I'd nip around corners, sure I'd seen the back of his coat, ready to beg him to have pity on me. I wrote him a letter. "I can't live without you. I want to live with you and your new lover; I'm willing to take care of the children, wash, cook. I won't ask anything, if only I can be close to you."

I was desperate. What can I say?

He didn't answer.

My final try came months later, around midnight. I decided to slash my wrists. I talked on the telephone with Helena for a long time but didn't tell her anything. I was drinking heavily that night, unusual for me, and I just needed to hear a familiar voice. She suspected nothing. When we hung up, I turned on my small tape deck and put on Marvin Gaye. I put the volume way up and played the song over and over. "I want you to want me, want me too, just like I want you." I lit nine white candles and turned off the light.

By candlelight I stripped my bed and put on white sheets to match the candles. I mixed myself another gin and tonic with lime, for it was a hot mid-August night. I mixed several more; gin was a drink I was not accustomed to and I didn't know its potency.

When the wax had run over the candlesticks and onto the table, I took a new razor blade from its container and cut deep into my left wrist. For a while I felt nothing, so I cut deeper.

I saw it before I felt it. Blood on the sheets, over the mattress, down the floor. I screamed. I stared at the blood and then at my wrist. It hurt like hell. I was going to faint. I staggered to the phone and called for help. I didn't mind dying, but, shit, I wasn't expecting it to hurt like that. So there I was on the ward again, getting patched up, waiting to get discharged. When I got home I threw out the pills I'd had to quiet my nerves. I was scared but had seen enough blood to make me never miss menstruating again.

Slowly I pulled my life and myself together. After all, it wasn't the end of the world. Just the end of a chapter with an endangered species whose manhood was at risk.

Today I still love weddings. Here I am, revelling in my cousin's future. There would be little Helenas and I'd get my chance to play part-time mother.

Compared to my wedding, Helena's was small. A handful of friends and family. Like I said, I was the only bridesmaid. The other attendant was the best man.

I wore a lovely floor-length two-piece red outfit. The skirt was long and tight-fitting, with a split in the back leading up to the beginning of my thighs. The sleeveless top sucked over my small but upright breasts; from the waist down the top fell generously over my high, firm bottom. My hair was braided in tiny plaits and held off my face by a lovely red band. The best man, Monty's cousin, wore a yellow three-piece suit a size too small for his large frame. His red tie matched my outfit and a white carnation poked out of the buttonhole on the left side of his jacket.

But I have to tell you, my cousin looked just lovely. Better than I'd ever seen her look before. Her gown was soft and sleeve-less: pure off-white silk. On her head was a small caplet from which flowed a white veil. That smile that could so easily turn into outrageous laughter showed perfectly white teeth. Standing there, she looked every bit the picture of virtue. Before the service began I hugged her and wished her good luck. She told me she loved me. Something in the touch of her hands made me look at her and lose myself in the beauty of her smile.

Monty wore a black three-piece suit, perfectly fitted, with a white shirt, a dark-green tie and a white carnation. His locks were caught loosely in an elastic band at the back of his neck.

Monty had wanted to marry in the Ethiopian Orthodox church, but Helena insisted she had to give her parents that one wish, so the Anglican church it was. The ceremony was longer than usual, for they had written their own vows. Monty was nervous, shifting from foot to foot as if his shoes were too tight. He even missed a few of his lines. Helena's voice was like the sound of a singing bird, sweet and clear. I would be a liar if I said I didn't cry tears of joy.

Then it was over and we drove to High Park to take the wedding pictures. Monty was himself again: easy-going, laid-back.

The camera snapped all evening: shots with Helena's parents, then with Monty's mother and sister, then me with the best man. It was glorious in the park but still very hot. Fortunately for Helena and me, our dresses were light.

By late evening it was cooler. The parents of the bride and groom left to get ready for the reception. The rest of us stayed back in the park, strolling around the flower beds, tossing confetti into the pond. I guess that was not ecologically sound, but it seemed like the thing to do.

It was almost dark when we drove off to my cousin's apartment for the reception. She had a tiny one-bedroom in a working-class Italian neighbourhood. It was above a Caribbean record shop on a busy street with cars and buses constantly on the move. The table was beautifully spread, with a white table cloth beneath the three-layer wedding cake decorated with white icing. At the top of the third cake stood a bride and groom made out of brown icing. The rest of the cake was covered with tiny yellow, red and green flowers. The ceiling and walls of the apartment were covered with red and yellow balloons. Oh it was heavenly, but the smell of the curried goat just about overpowered the small apartment.

The speeches were long, with some embarrassing moments for my cousin and her new husband. It was, however, a festive occasion. After a few glasses of rum punch, my uncle swallowed hard and made the final speech about his baby girl, whose diapers he'd once changed. He was almost in tears by the time he got to the part where she first called him Papa and took her first steps into his arms. Through it all, my beautiful cousin sat calmly and patiently, never showing a hint of discomfort, that wonderful smile on her face. It was hard to believe that this was the same girl who had pissed in the department store, driven madly without a license to Niagara Falls, stripped and danced for pleasure from Calgary to Montreal to Las Vegas.

Finally it was time for the bride and groom to dance the first song of the night. I then danced with the groom and my cousin with the best man. The parents left shortly after. Soon we were in the heat of the party, shaking to the beat of the music.

When the last guest left, I stayed behind to help clean up. We smoked a couple of joints and picked crumbs of icing from the remainder of the wedding cake. I didn't much feel like moving from the couch, but it was their wedding night, so I reached towards the phone to call a taxi.

"What you doing?" asked Monty, casually. "Just stay over tonight. Why spend good money on a cab?" I was caught off guard and looked over at my cousin. Helena herself looked a little taken aback, but she was her old self in no time. That smile was on her face. And even I could not decipher what it meant.

"Yeah, relax. It's not like Monty and I never spent a night alone. Goodness, we've been sleeping together for the last three months." I stood up, looking at them both, still dialing for the taxi. Helena reached over and took the phone from me, hanging up. I felt some embarrassment and moved toward the door.

"No, really, stay." She held on to my arm. "Stay."

Helena helped me pull open the sofa bed then went into the bedroom to bring sheets. Monty was leaning over me, "Why don't you join us in bed?"

I looked at him, giving him a forced smile, which actually meant are you a crazy fucker or what. Then I heard my cousin's voice, "Don't be a stranger. The bed's big enough, come on."

I couldn't read her tone—to this day I can't describe it. But I wasn't a young girl with high hopes or morals, so I went in the bedroom, and they made space for me in the middle of the bed. I still had on my red dress as I slipped under the covers. My cousin wore only her bra and panties. Monty was naked except for his underpants. I felt over-dressed and uncomfortable, yet I was secretly excited. This was out of the ordinary. Perverse in some way. We talked a bit about the wedding, the embarrassing speeches, the delicious food, the fantastic party . . . and then there wasn't anything left to talk about.

I was grateful when Helena offered me a T-shirt, I relaxed a bit. Monty handed me a joint and a glass of the rum punch. We talked about who had drunk too much and who hadn't drunk enough and then I fell asleep to the sounds of the cars and buses below. I woke up to a warm firm hand caressing my breast and thought I was in a dream. I enjoyed it. It was Helena's hand travelling as she slept. Then the hand became bolder and my legs were parted and met with a beard and moustache. This wasn't cousin Helena. My cousin's new husband was pulling my panties to the side. I turned towards my cousin. I tightened my legs and bottom, protesting silently. His body closed in on my behind. I pressed closer to my cousin. She must have felt me shift, for her eyes opened and she turned around to catch hold of her husband's hand still tugging at my panties.

"What's the matter with this husband of yours?" I tried to sound light. "I'm going," I said, jumping towards my clothes bundled up on a chair nearby.

"Forget it, stay. It's too late to be going out. He's just a lousy fuckin' dog. Just my luck."

She reached over to the night table for her pack of cigarettes. "Here, have one."

Monty was bold. He reached over to her and pulled her mouth to his. She didn't resist. He whispered something to her. I didn't hear. I was pulling hard on my cigarette. He was pulling the strap of her bra.

I was not sure what was going on, was this a ménage à trois? "Let's have another drink and a real smoke," said Monty in an unusually talkative voice.

"I'm going. I think I've had enough for one day," I said in a very high voice. I looked over to my cousin for some help.

"Stay," she said. "Let's have a drink, a joint. I'll even roll it."

I was confused. Was she accommodating Monty, or was she being entertained? Did he know about her past adventures?

Monty came back with three glasses of rum. I had a sip but

could drink no more. I was beginning to see shadows of things that weren't in the room, gaudy carnival booths, riding a ferris wheel that wouldn't stop. Monty put on a Nina Simone album, one he knew was a favourite of ours. We smoked the joint slowly and he drank his rum quickly, going back for a second.

Now he was in the middle. He addressed my cousin, with a boyish grin. "You didn't give me a wedding present, you know." She looked at him in a strange sort of way. Then that quick smile covered her pretty face. I kept smoking, perhaps a little faster, wanting to feel relaxed and very high.

She sat staring at him. The night was hot and she had thrown the covers off, showing her breasts. She lit another cigarette.

"How about giving me your cousin as a wedding present?" It was as if I weren't in the room. What had she told him?

The room was still for a while, except for Nina Simone, going on about a thin gold ring, or something like that. It was dark too, except for the street lights outside, but still I could see when my cousin reached over and kissed him passionately. Unpredictable, that cousin of mine. But I loved her as much as I loved weddings.

His hand had no problem in finding my breast. I didn't pull away. But when his hands again tried to part my legs, I tugged at my cousin to say or do something. Helena just shrugged. She leaned over Monty to me, her breast at my cheek. In a calm controlled voice she asked, "Do you mind fucking with him? My wedding present?"

"It's up to you, Helena," I said. "I didn't give you a present, did I?" I joked, "so if this is what you want, then it's fine by me." I tried to sound bold.

"Yeah. If this is the present he wants, let's make him happy." She laughed that nervy laugh. "Let's make it memorable." I searched her eyes for some answer to this bizarre turn of events, but found none.

He wasted no time.

Monty groped for my crotch, hoisting himself on top of me. He clumsily tried to shove his rapidly softening cock inside me. My cousin played with the tiny braids on my head. I was beginning to enjoy this when a warm liquid poured over my face and breasts. A foul, sour smell. I cursed. My cousin jumped up and turned on the light.

"Fuckin' jerk! Bastard! You want women and you can't even give a good fuck. Didn't just want me. Wanted my cousin. Asshole!" Her voice was loud, angry and full. I wondered again why she went along with it and why she married him in the first place.

Monty sat on the side of the bed in his own vomit. I felt almost sorry for him. But it was Helena's wedding night too, and she didn't ask for this. I slipped out of bed for the quiet and security of the bathroom.

I showered quickly. My cousin was dressed when I opened the bathroom door. Dressed in her wedding dress, complete with veil. I found this weird, but what the hell, so was the rest of the night. I quickly dressed in my crumpled red bridesmaid's dress.

"Come on, let's go," she commanded. "I can't stand it in here."

Monty didn't say a word. He sat there looking the fool. Or cool. Or the deep thinker. I don't know.

We left the apartment, walked down the street. "Let's have a drink," she said. It was way past bar hours, but we knew of several after-hours joints nearby, so arm in arm we walked toward Monroe's.

Cars slowed down to watch us, Helena in her bridal gown and veil, and me, rumpled but dressed to kill in red.

When we walked into Monroe's, the customers stared at us. The bartender came over to see if we were all right. Just fine, we assured him. No problem. We switched from the sweet syrup of the rum punch to double scotches.

"Let's drink a toast," laughed Helena. "A toast to that fuckin' bastard, my lawful wedded husband. What did the minister say?

'Till death do us part'? Fuck him. Fuck the minister too."

Our glasses clinked.

"Two more shots of scotch," my cousin Helena shouted to the bartender. Marvin Gaye was singing the song I had played when I slashed my wrist.

"Let's dance, cous." We danced, Marvin in our ears. The men looked on at us. We danced long and slow.

BABY

Asha woke up to find Baby close. Her nipple was sore from Baby's hunger of the night before. She was tired, her eyes red from too much crying. She eased Baby away, so as not to wake her. Asha left the bedroom and walked down the hall to the bathroom, avoiding a small stain on the carpet. Shit, one of the cats must have vomited last night.

Downstairs in the kitchen, she made herself a cup of coffee and curled up on the sofa with Mooney, the oldest cat. She had five. Mooney was almost seventeen years old.

She was a sucker for cats. A stray only had to come to the front door or the back yard a few times, with an unkept look, hungry eyes, and she would take it in. Friends teased her often.

"Girl, you should have been a vet, you have no business wasting your time as a school teacher, look at all dem hundreds of strays just waiting for a home. If we had money girl, we would done set you up on a farm." They would laugh, rolling their eyes at each other as if she were the strangest person they had ever met.

She got up from the couch, fed the cats and helped herself to another cup of coffee, this time adding ice. It was daybreak, but she could already feel the approaching heat. The cats circled her, some at her feet, others on the couch. When Asha got up they followed her to the half-open kitchen window.

"Dammit, why am I so absentminded? I have to remember to close this damn window at nights," she mumbled to herself as the cats dashed through. Asha paused and whispered a silent prayer: "Thank God, this isn't back home. They would have climbed in and stolen every goddam thing but the cats."

She needed to be active, take her mind off last night. Doing housework gave her time to think. She washed towels, sheets and a basket of Baby's clothing. By noon she had changed the cat litter, washed the pots and dishes from the night before, and swept and washed the kitchen floor, working up a bucket of sweat.

Asha felt worn, but still she craved the closeness of Baby. She wanted to lie next to her. To listen to her quiet breath and to feel Baby turn lips to breast.

She went back to bed and stripped to her panties; it was going to be a hot one. Oblivious to the heat and still half asleep, Baby reached for Asha's breast. Despite the soreness and the slight bruise, Asha gave in to her, and feeling a sudden warmth come over her body, she slowly drifted in and out of sleep, barely noticing Baby's pull.

It had been an early night. They'd had supper. Fed the cats. Settled upstairs in bed to watch television. A few sitcoms, a game show, a mystery.

Kneeling in front of Baby, Asha had gently undressed her and stroked her with her tongue.

"I would die for you," said one. Said the other, "I would kill for you."

Passion talk.

Love talk.

Woman talk.

It doesn't matter who said what.

With Baby so close, Asha felt grateful for the privacy Canada had given them. Sleepless, she stood in front of the window, looking out. The moon loomed high. The maple tree outside the window, with its full green protective canopy, made her ache for home. No paradise but full of life. She missed the loud dance hall music pushing itself through closed doors, the boisterous talk in the streets, the boys hanging out on the street corner, the sudden knock on the door from an unexpected friend. No maple trees, but fruit trees of every size and description: mango, coconut, orange, papaya, all luscious. Naseberry, guava, sweetsop, and sugar cane, she could almost taste it, juice so s . . . sweet. Oh, what joy, what pain, that sugar cane. Turning to molasses, turning to rum, turning to export, sweetening white tongues while black tongues taste ash.

Asha was pulled out of her thoughts by a sudden scream from Baby. Baby sat upright, a sour look on her face.

"What's the matter, Baby?" Asha asked, concerned.

"I had another bad dream. I can't take them anymore. It's the same one. Do you love me, Asha?"

"Baby, you know I do; why are you asking me this?"

"The dream, it comes every now and then, it's always the same. We are in a parade, dressed up in masks, costumes . . . and then you disappear on me. I can't find you anywhere." Baby sulked.

"Baby, it's only a dream; you know I won't leave you. Not now, not ever."

Baby jumped up suddenly from the bed, chased the cats out of the room, cursing each one by name, and slammed the bedroom door.

Asha sat quietly, watching Baby.

"We have to talk, Asha. We have to talk about us. I can't go on like this."

Asha got up quietly and lit two candles to aid the moon's glow as it crept through the window. In the flicker of the candle-light, Baby's eyes sparked anger and determination.

"We have to talk, I tell you. SOMETHING is wrong with our relationship. That dream is about us." Baby's voice went higher. "Talk to me, talk to me!" she demanded. "We go nowhere together, excepting the Hotspot Restaurant, which don't count. We hardly have any friends. All we do is watch TV. It's like I'm invisible in your life . . . " She was now pacing the floor. She waited for a response, but Asha just sat, staring at no place in particular.

"This goddam TV. Aaah, I wish I were a violent person. You know what I'd do?" Baby paused, and with no reply from Asha, she went on. "I'd kick the shit out of it and throw it through this goddam window.

"Asha, we can't go on like this. I want out. Do you hear me? O-U-T. Out. Watch my mouth, I want to live like a normal person, not in a closet."

Asha's face was hidden behind a glass of water. "What do you mean, Baby?" she asked, just to fill the silence.

What Baby could not express in words she said by raking her hands over Asha's face. "Stop it," Asha commanded. "Let's talk, but don't pounce on me like some animal." Then, her voice soft, she asked, "Why are you turning on me, Baby? We were fine a few hours ago. Don't let the dream do this."

Baby replied in a voice as heavy and dark as the night outside, "These dreams mean something, Asha. They don't just come from no place. They're in my head and my head don't lie. You know what I mean. You do nothing but watch TV. When was the last time we went to the movies? Or to a women's bar? Or to a party at one of my friends' house? We've never even gone to a damn gay pride parade. Every time I ask you to go out, it's 'Oh

Baby, there's a good program on TV tonight.' Or 'Oh Baby, you know I hate the bars.'"

It was Asha's turn to say something. "Baby, you know I don't like the bars, it's not a lie. I don't like the smoke. Have I ever stopped you from going?"

"Who wants to fucking go out alone? My lover is home watching TV and I'm out all alone. What about bingo? What was your excuse last month? Oh yeah, you didn't like gambling. Then the movie, a clean wholesome environment, with popcorn and a soft drink? 'Oh Baby, that will come on TV soon.' Christ, Asha. I'm only thirty-five years old. I'm not ready for the cobwebs to start growing on me."

She stopped there, waiting for Asha to say she'd try to change. Asha said nothing.

"Say something, dammit. Look, you don't even respond. Sometimes I just want to walk out of this house and never look back."

Asha was sitting up in bed, her eyes filling with tears. She tried to pull Baby close.

"Don't touch me, DON'T. If you can't talk to me, don't touch me. You think you can cry a few tears, and everything will be okay, don't you? I should be the one crying. My name is Baby, isn't it?" she goaded. "No, Asha, I can't cry, that's reserved for you. My well-cultured, well-classed high school teacher, and that elegant face all dipped in milk chocolate." Baby stopped now, her smile sharp.

"Isn't it interesting, every time we have a quarrel, you throw my class, my education and my colour in my face. Why is it only when we disagree that they become a cross?" Asha demanded, her face now bitter chocolate.

A look of satisfaction rushed over Baby's face. She'd cut deep.

"Well, I'm packing." Baby began pulling sweaters and jeans out of drawers. "I'm tired of this closet. You enjoy it with the cats."

"I know what I am," continued Baby. "I'm a lesbian. A zami. A sodomite. A black-skinned woman. I got no education or family behind my name. I'm just a woman getting by. Asha, I'm ready for war. And you? You're ready to protect the little you have. Your job. Well, for me it just isn't enough."

Asha bent over to touch Baby's hands.

"Baby, some of what you say is true, but it's unfair for you to throw class at me every time we fight. And tell me, Baby, do I run back to class for shelter? You are so critical of me. I can't please you, everything I do is wrong. Baby, please try to understand. I love my work. I am a good teacher, and the Black students need that model. They need to see us in positive roles. They need to see more than the pimps-prostitutes-junkies. You know if the school finds out I'm a lesbian, they'll find a reason to get rid of me. And don't even talk about the parents." She was desperately trying to elicit some response from Baby.

Baby had piled the sweaters and jeans on the floor and was grabbing more clothes out of the closet and throwing them into a suitcase. Asha grabbed her. "Baby, listen to me. Don't leave. We belong together. We've been together for three years. Why now, why break up now?"

"I can't take it any longer, Asha. I can't. We can't go on gay demos because someone from school might see you on TV. We can't do this, we can't do that. I'm tired. I don't want to live like this. I can't stop my life because some people hate Blacks. And I am bloody well not going to stop living my life because another group hates lesbians. No job will ever keep me in the closet."

"Baby, are you saying I should just quit my job? Just walk out in the name of being a Black lesbian?"

"For God's sake, Asha, don't be so fucking dramatic. Live your life how you want. Stay in your closet. Me, I need fresh air. And if I have to fight for the right to enjoy it, then I will."

"I'm not being dramatic, Baby. But what do you want me to do? Just go in tomorrow morning and say 'Hey principal, hey fellow teachers, hey students, look at me. I'm a lesbian, have been all my life, just thought I should let you know.' Is that what you want?"

"Asha, sometimes I don't know you. Honest to God. Who are you hiding from?" Her voice became softer. "Asha, I love you. I want you to start living. I want us to start living."

Baby was the first to hear the sound outside the bedroom door.

"It's only the cats, Baby," Asha reassured her. "They want to be in here with us, to feel everything is all right." In a softer tone she added, "Baby, they don't like it when we fight, when we get unhappy." Asha pulled her close to kiss her. Baby didn't pull back. They dropped to the pile of clothes on the floor.

The man standing outside the bedroom door had come into the house through the kitchen window. He was of average height. He had black curly hair, cut close to his scalp. The right side of his mouth pulled up in a nervous twitch. He wore a pair of navy blue cotton shorts and a plain white cotton T-shirt. He wore no mask. He had a white plastic bag in his hand.

He was no stranger, had lived next door in a rooming house for the past year, but was planning to go out West any day now. The women knew him, too. They didn't know his name, but he was a familiar face in the Hotspot, where they sometimes went to eat or have a beer. The Hotspot served as a hangout for locals. It carried a good Caribbean menu, Caribbean beers and rum. The Hotspot was always jammed—jobless neighbours dropped in on the way back from one more no-go interview. The ones with jobs came to cash a cheque, the hangers-on were there all day, waiting to strike it big in the lottery. The juke box never stopped playing. The back room housed gamblers and folks with items to sell.

Some of the regular customers paid little notice to the two women who always came together. Others talked about them. The man hung around the Hotspot after work and on weekends,

drinking beer and looking for a way to get in on the con\
tions of the regulars.

"When I win di lottery, I going home to soak up some of a
sun, buy a nice house, car and find myself a good woman."

"My boss man is like a slave driver. I can't even take a leak
without the supervisor coming to look for me."

"They lay me off after twenty-five years' service and tell me
times rough."

"Bwoy, dem girls different. Dem need a good fuck. Can't understand how nice Black woman like dem get influence in dis
lesbian business."

"Nastiness man, nastiness. Satan work."

He'd overheard the last comment many times. He'd watched
the two women closely each time they came into the Hotspot.
They had an independent streak about them. He didn't like it.
They come to Canada and they adopt foreign ways, he thought
to himself.

He stood silently outside their bedroom door now, fingering the
shiny black gun he had removed from its plastic bag. It was a .38
calibre automatic he'd bought from a stranger at the Hotspot
Restaurant. The seller was looking for cash, had to leave town in
a hurry. The man had the money. "Why not?" he'd said. Tonight
he was going to put a stop to all this nastiness. He'd try to help
them, and if they didn't listen, then they'd have to face the con-
sequences. God never intended them to be this way. God wanted
man and woman together.

"Oh, Baby, I don't want you to leave me," whispered Asha.
"Love me forever, Baby. Don't stop."

"I won't. But Asha, save some of this for later. Don't let the
well run dry," Baby teased.

He could hear it all through the closed door. The gun was
getting warm and sticky in his hand. The front of his shorts

jumped like a trapped crab.

"What do you want me to do, Asha?"

"Baby, you know what I like best." Without another word, she pushed Baby's head down.

The crab jumped higher. He switched the gun from hand to hand. He wanted to fire it through the door. He took the crab out of his pants to give it room. It was hard. He played with it, pulling and squeezing it.

Bitches, sluts, ungodly creatures. He intended to tie them up. Strap their legs against each other. Oh, he was going to teach them a lesson. Let them do those things to each other right before his eyes.

He was excited, the crab more restless, the gun hot in his hand. Tie up them lezzies. Then fuck them. Let them feel what it's like to get fucked by a real man. He wished he had carried his knife so he could slit their throats, watch the red running down their tits.

The crab throbbed.

Bitches. Let the dirty bitches feel the real thing. He might even let one of them feel it in her mouth.

When he was finished with their bodies, he would rob them, take their money and jewellery. Use the silencer. Do a good clean job, then leave through the kitchen window. He'd already packed his few belongings. Leave early morning on the Greyhound bus. He was tired of his job as a security guard in the stinking rotten high-rise building in downtown Toronto anyway. He'd had enough of Toronto and its dirty filthy morals, its dirty filthy women, dirty filthy life. Things were different in Vancouver, he'd heard. Nice people, nice open land. Mountains and ocean. That's what he needed. A place like back home. A place big enough that he wouldn't have to see women like these, his own people, stooping to this.

Standing at the bedroom door, he was reminded of conversations he'd picked up on at the Hotspot.

"I would like to fuck dem girls. Give it to dem good in di ass."

"Ass, boy? I want to throw dem legs over di shoulder and pump everything in."

"Dem gal need to learn lessons. Man fi woman and woman fi man. None of this nastiness, none of this separation."

The cats had come upstairs. They sat staring at him. He couldn't stand the goddam creatures. Hated their fur and their tongues.

"Can't stand the bitches," he muttered, wanting to use the gun.

He could hear Asha and Baby clearly. Ignoring the cats as best as he could, he turned his mind to the crab. It couldn't wait. He jerked it back and forth, leaving a small puddle on the red carpet, only partly muffling the grunt that came from his mouth.

"Those damn cats," Baby muttered.

"Leave them alone, Baby. They're just playing. In fact, they're watching over us. They're our guard cats."

Asha and Baby had tumbled off the pile of clothes, wrapped around each other.

He stayed outside. The crab had gone to sleep and he was getting tired. They were so loud. Bitches. He'd give them a few more minutes. Wait for them to start up again, then he would kick down the door and watch them.

"Asha, this doesn't change anything, you know."

"What do you mean, Baby? What do you want me to do?"

"I love you, Asha, but this isn't the Middle Ages. For God's sake, get involved in a gay group for teachers, or something. I just can't live like this. I won't live like this. I'm tired, Asha."

He was getting impatient. Too much arguing. He wished he had kicked the door in earlier. He should have done it when the crab was awake. He'd never wake it now.

The gun went back into the plastic bag. He walked down the stairs and climbed out through the kitchen window.

WELFARE LINE

I am standing in the welfare line. The place crowded like hell. The cheque didn't come. All the chairs in the place full up. All kinds of people in the line. The one at the beginning of the line is Indian like me, but from the sound of her voice, she come from one of dem African countries, maybe Kenya. Don't sound like any part of India or Pakistan. We look alike, but I'm from Jamaica.

Some Blacks sitting in chairs too. Some look African, others look Caribbean, and di one talking have a Canadian accent. Some Native people here and other people from China and Korea. Lots of poor whites too. Some of dem look drunk and drug-out. Bwoy, is like a conference of the United Nations right here. Dem sitting around talking, some sulky. Coffee and donut all around.

Two guys behind me just mek me laugh, forgetting how much

I hate standing in this line. One telling the other how to deal with the girl at the counter. Seem like dis is him first time here.

"They're going to ask you everything. They want to know all about your life. Don't be surprised if they ask you for your favourite sex position."

Dem keep me entertain the whole time in the line. Dem sound like college people. Business college types. Talking about computers: DOS, dis, dat, WordPerfect, IBM, Mac. I don't really understand it all. Dem just like the kinds I met when I enrol in that business course in night school at Atkinson College. To tell the truth, the conversation was a relief from all else around me. The place pack. Is Christmas and people vex because dem have no money and the stores full of Christmas goods. Dem have children to buy gifts for, and turkey and ham for the table, liquor for the season. Make some rum punch and steam a nice Christmas pudding, invite some friends over, play some music. Some Otis Redding, Sarah Vaughan and reggae. Mi don't too like all this new music, dis dancehall, rap ting. Give me Toots any day.

The one in front of me is a Filipina woman, just come to Canada it seem. Maybe a refugee? Come to think of it, all of us is refugee, come here for one reason or another. Adopt all kinds of name and identity to stay on.

I hear the clerk talking to her. "Do you speak English? I don't understand you. What is your name?"

"Name?"

The poor woman confused and the clerk is getting vex and rude. Then a man who look Filipino hear the confusion and come over same time to help. Him start to talk to the woman in their language. Di woman face relax.

The line stretch way out on the street in the cold. Mi so glad mi come early because I couldn't take that cold outside. Then to put up with dem blasted people who think dem shit don't stink, looking on as dem drive by. I sure some of dem same ones use to collect welfare.

Mi never see this place so crowded before. We all so close together that we smelling one another and mistaking it for weself.
Is four days before Christmas. People hungry. We want to get
clean up, fix up our place, dress up, eat and drink. Celebrate the
holidays like normal people. But see here, listen how mi start
talking like we not normal because we standing in the welfare
line. I am next to deal with the woman behind the welfare
counter. There is a Black woman before me.

"What kind of Christmas I going to have? No money to buy
anything for my children," the woman was muttering.

I catch her Jamaican accent. She definitely street-smart. She
not raising her voice to the counter woman, and she standing
straight up, no slumping, and she looking right into the woman
face. She dress tidy, like she work in the place, like she really understand this welfare thing and the people behind the counter.
Her voice rise sometimes, but it come off more forceful than
shrill and frighten. You have to be that way to deal with this welfare business, or they take advantage of you. Some of them love
to talk to you like you don't have any sense.

"I can't do anything about that. You'll get your cheque in the
mail."

The Jamaican woman say, "But what about the holidays? No
mail don't come and I need to buy things for . . . "

"Just mail it in."

Then is as if the woman lose her cool. She not composed any
more.

"Bumbo claat!" she shout loud, for everyone to hear. The
place get quiet. She continue, "So dis is Canada, hard like ice.
You people tink only certain a unnu must enjoy Christmas?"
She sucked her teeth.

The woman behind the counter motions to me. "Next."

"YES, SEND IT IN DI MAIL, and a Merry Christmas to you
too." She turns to go, almost knocking me out of the line.

"These rass claat people," she says loudly, "want to see you suffer, even on Christmas Day."

"Come," she addresses a little boy waiting among the crowd. "Come mek we go. Don't cry, dem can't spoil our holiday." She leaves with a string of cuss words trailing behind her.

My turn. I'm at the glass window, talking soft. I don't want nobody in my business, but the blasted woman keep saying, "Lady, I can't hear you. Will you speak louder. Date of birth?"

I get hot in the face, but it don't look like anybody paying much attention. These questions standard and not a soul care.

"The eight of the ninth, 1946," I say.

"Speak louder, please. I don't have all day."

She not looking up at me at all, just asking the questions.

"Worker?"

"Mam, I don't remember his name."

She looks up for the first time.

With nuff irritation in her voice, like she addressing a child, "I don't need his name. You know we don't use workers' names. I need your worker's number." Di girl mek mi feel like a damn fool.

"I'm sorry, mam, I don't remember his number. Is a long time I don't come to the office. My cheque always come to my house in the mail, but they change my worker and ask me to come in."

"Well, you obviously did not come in immediately, which is why no cheque was mailed to you."

She leafs through a book in front of her.

"Your worker is Number 72. Please try to remember it. You'll have to wait."

These rass people, they feel because you in a little difficulty and collecting temporary welfare that you married to them. They call and they want you to drop everything to come down to this place. To sit and wait and wait. Cinderella don't have anything over us here.

The new worker come out. Is a man. Maybe I will have better luck with him. "Ma'am, are you landed?"

"Children?"

"How many?"

"Do you have a passport?"

"Birth certificates for the children?"

"Name of the father?"

"Divorced ten years, you say? Sorry ma'am, that doesn't matter. I still need those papers."

"Do you know his whereabouts?"

"It doesn't matter if he's not living in Canada. If he is in India, we'll find him."

To rahtid. If I didn't need the money mi woulda did jus walk out. India. Blasted wrenk idiot. So everybody who is Indian born in India?

"The kids are Canadian-born? Sorry, ma'am, I still need their birth certificates."

"You're a Canadian citizen? Sorry, I still need to see proof of landed status."

Is what dis man a deal wid? Immigration papers and him see mi passport.

"Bank account?"

"Rent receipts?"

"Sir, I showed all this to my last worker five months ago."

Him straighten him glasses and look dead in mi face.

"Sir, I don't have all of those papers with me; I didn't walk with them. Can I bring them in after the Christmas?"

"I don't make the rules around here."

Him ask mi to wait while him check de computer. Mi get out of the cubbyhole and go back outside. No seat to sit down. Chairs full of people waiting. Walls full of slumped bodies, waiting for a cheque, waiting to get out. Some tired-looking, just slouching in the chairs, half asleep. Others bouncing with energy, looking for anybody to talk to.

I wonder how I look. Me with a little piece of scarf to hold down my hair. Jeans and runners. A thick black cotton jacket. Funny thing, nobody really care.

We all just want to get out. Mi so hot in my coat, but nowhere to hang it. Safer still on mi back. It protect mi from the smell of de stale coffee and de occasional fart that pass now and then through the room, smelling like four-day-old boiled eggs and stale wet rice.

"Okay, ma'am. Everything seems to be in order, I checked the information on the computer. Sorry for the long wait," he apologized. "What's the problem?"

"My cheque didn't come."

"Well, why didn't you come in sooner?"

"I was sick and couldn't come."

"You should have come anyway."

I look down into my lap, picking at my fingernails. For the truth is, I was sick bad, I couldn't even get out of bed.

The bastard must have felt some pity for the way I look. "Okay, wait. I'll get a cheque ready for you."

Outside in the cold, I search through my handbag for busfare. My next stop is to pick up some toys, clothes and a few groceries. I walk into the Children's Aid building to pick up the toys and clothes, hoping is not another long line-up.

Is only three people in front of me.

"Take all you want, lady."

This is a surprise. Sure different from that welfare office.

The clothes look good. The label read Cotton Somebody— something like that. Mi tek a bundle of sweaters, a few pair of pants, two winter jackets and some shorts, though is winter. They give me a garbage bag and I fill it up with all the clothes, a few running shoes. The lady try to fill me up with more summer things and toys. I take them all. I will send some to Jamaica. Nothing wasted.

I walk to the nearest subway station. My next stop before home is the food bank.

The subway pack. People everywhere with big shopping bags— Simpsons, Eaton's, The Bay all about. I get a seat eventually and sit down. Mi get tired of reading the ads on the train, and of the quiet. Our Christmas back home is boss, singing and jollification everywhere. The train like a funeral home, so I start to open some of the packages they give me at the Children's Aid. All white dolls coming out of these packages. Everything white. White Barbie, white Ken. So mi begin to talk to miself about all this whiteness around me and in the bag. Some people in the train staring, but I don't care. After standing in the welfare line today I'm entitled to talk to myself. Is my garbage bag. Is my business.

So let dem look with dem starchy face.

The food bank is another long line. This time I don't escape the outdoors, the cold and the slush, for the line go on and on. I pick up a tin of ham, a chicken and some canned food.

Tomorrow I will have to get some more food. Go to the Caribbean shops. Go down to Kensington market and get the other things that di food bank don't supply: coconut, green banana, goat for the curry, some red peas. Sorrel and some music. Can't celebrate the season without music. We have to play the devil, play the music, play the fool.

CARMELLA

Carmella. I put the letter back in its envelope and smiled to myself. She hadn't changed. Not one bit. Off on another adventure, this time to explore the home of Anne of Green Gables. Though she didn't actually say that. That's not her style, and anyway, that would be just too corny. She didn't talk like that. The corniest thing she ever said was, "Oh for God's sake, please." And that isn't that corny, is it? It's kind of cool, as my daughters would say.

For the last ten years, she had been passing through every province in Canada. I wasn't surprised that she was planning to settle down in Prince Edward Island.

It's very tropical. Very much small-island. I hope it's never discovered, like Vancouver, or Banff, which I think is overrated. This is the place to be.

She was forever the trend-maker. Always blazing ahead. Seeking out new places. Squeezing excitement out of anything just ordinary and normal. I poured some diet soda and arranged myself in a comfortable chair in front of the television. I stifled a second smile, actually a weary one. I could just hear Carmella's voice: "Oh for God's sake, don't tell me you've bought into this diet shit. Free up. What's this shit?"

But Carmella was different, she didn't have a husband who reminded her of her one-hundred-and-ten-pound figure before the three children. She didn't have in-laws that clipped fitness articles for her from *Chatelaine* and *Essence* magazines. She didn't have three teenage daughters who never bothered to steal her clothes because they would only be baggy where they should be tight. I envied her, though she had been my best friend for twenty-five years.

I had arrived in Toronto just eight weeks before I met her. We were both taking night classes at a nearby high school. I was taking a typing course, so I could get into secretarial school, and she, English and history. Said she wanted to go to university, was going to write. Something like that. I remembered her saying, "I want to be a writer. A poet."

I must admit that was what attracted me to her. All those highfalutin ideas, as my mother would say. Me, I wanted to find office work. A nine-to-five job, with enough time left for me to party and shop. No studying at night. I figured I'd done enough of that as a girl living at home with my parents. I just wanted my pay cheque. Punching a keyboard and answering the telephone. Pushing paper, that was the ideal.

I wasn't into high activity: my ancestors had had enough of that to last me a lifetime. While I was attending night school, my mother was still cleaning offices at night. No, I wanted to sit in those offices. When I got my first job, in an insurance company, I didn't find the two coffee breaks, the lunch hour, the ritual, boring. Not at all.

Carmella, though, cursed it every chance she got. "Oh for God's sake! How can you do that every day?" She just shook her head when I told her that my ambition was to settle down with a nice guy and have two kids, a car and maybe a dog. "Hey, don't knock it," I had challenged her. "It could be a good life. You can go on with your high ideals, your independence, your great art."

So Carmella was my extreme opposite. Yet we fit together like cup and saucer. I led her to dances and parties, and she took me to readings and writers' get-togethers. Sometimes she took me to parties where people sat with glasses of wine and talked books. I couldn't understand it at all. I got to taking a cassette tape with me. At times I would just put on my tape and start dancing in the middle of their fancy talk: the muse, the genre, demonic possessions. What bullshit! When we left the party, she would go on, "Oh for God's sake, did you have to play that music?"

"Why? What was wrong with it?" I would innocently ask.

"Oh, let's not bother," she would end, tired and defeated.

Our times together were not always so disagreeable, and I got to like her books. She was a great reader. Some time after night school we found an apartment and moved in together. By then I was working at the insurance company and she was studying at university. Some nights, after her classes we would grab a beer and a pizza and she would read poetry aloud. Most nights I enjoyed the poetry, her voice, so soft and soothing. When the poetry got too much to take, I escaped to an after-hours joint with one of my boyfriends. She came sometimes, but it was always, "Oh God, girl, how can you stand this dark hole? And the music just don't make no sense. All this machismo shit, how can you listen to it?"

We continued to live together in the apartment for five years. With many a fight, for though it was a two-bedroom, she always made it her business to criticize my boyfriends. "Oh God, how can you stand these men? Please, what about aesthetics?"

"I am just an ordinary girl," I would answer. She did not value the practical things about some men—like their ability to fix a faucet, paint walls or repair the stereo! She was into pretty faces, smooth talk and classy dress.

"Look," she would say to me, "my mother chose a practical man, and where did it get her?"

I didn't contradict her, but I agreed with her mother, even if she did end up with many children.

Carmella would go on and on, and then in a deadly serious tone she would say, "Girl, give me muscle, I just want plain, old-fashion muscles." That would have us falling about, laughing.

We generally got on well. We were both from working-class families, with mothers who cleaned people's houses, and neither of us knew our fathers. We both had many brothers and sisters. Some we knew, some we didn't. Carmella wasn't about to repeat her mother's life. I loved children, and, I have to admit, I wanted a husband, two rings on my left hand, a nice house and all that. I just didn't want to clean other people's floors, or to care for half a dozen kids and fight with half a dozen babies' fathers.

Carmella loved sports. The works: football, baseball, hockey. The rougher the sport, the more she enjoyed watching it. God, she even liked boxing. I wasn't that type. The roughest sport I wanted to get into was on the dance floor or in the comfort of my bedroom. She shared her love of sports with my boyfriends. And despite her cursing about my men, she could sit down with them, discuss football and drink scotch. They pretty much liked her. The only time they didn't was when she insisted on reading poetry. She had no sense of the moment and would get upset every time one of my boyfriends fell asleep. Her own dates pretended to be interested, but I could always tell that they would rather be up close to her. They rarely ever made it under the covers with her. They were showpieces, seldom lovers.

Still, she made a difference in my life. She was determined not to be what she called the typical Caribbean person. Didn't want to be wedged into any stereotype. She would always complain,

"Those people at school—those mothers—they think we know nothing: we can't speak proper English, we have no interests other than our own world and families." She could go on and she often did.

I thought she was trying too hard to prove to them that she was just as good, if not better. Me, fuck them. I wasn't about to spend my time studying at the university to prove to them that I had a brain and that I knew literature, their literature. I wasn't going to spend my life trying to pronounce words I couldn't even spell, written by men I knew nothing about and had even less interest in. I'd rather spend my time mastering the winding and grinding of a dance, tying and untying a turban, discovering the length and breadth of the after-hours clubs.

Darling Eve, it is heavenly here. You can actually see the stars. The sound of the ocean thrills me, leaves me speechless, if you can believe that. My writing is going well; did you receive the review of my book I sent you? National paper—not bad, eh?

Anyway, enough about me. How are the kids—and Delroy? Kids! here I go again, but they do grow up so quickly I can't keep track.

I've met some fantastic women out here. Pity you hadn't run off with me to see the country, it's so wonderful. But then you wouldn't have met the man of your dreams and had all those wonderful children, would you? Give my love to Delroy, he's a very lucky man.

...I picked up some young man that I slept with once. He bored me. I think I'd rather be celibate. I just want to write, though I sometimes fear how isolated I might become. I don't imagine I will ever settle with a man, not at my age ... I'm too settled in my ways—my books, my writing, the ocean.

When we took the apartment we had long ago decided we would be as different as we could from our families: no housecleaning on Saturday; no cooking every day; no washing once a week. Let the dishes pile up, the garbage overflow. What difference would it make to our lives, we declared, if we cleaned every day?

After a few months of our practising this philosophy and living in what could be politely considered a pigsty, Carmella came up with a brilliant idea. I could never have dreamed it up.

"Why don't we get an agency to send a worker over to our apartment? She could do the washing, clean up the apartment."

"Yes," I said eagerly, "why didn't we think of this a long time ago?"

We checked with agencies for rates, and calculated the fee. A full day's work would come to what we earned in half a day at our jobs. Convinced by our excitement, we talked about it all night. "Why didn't we think of this before?" asked Carmella. "We relieve ourselves of this work, and we pay a woman who really needs the money."

"Let's support our own," we pledged.

In the morning we called an agency that had a range of cleaners from the Third World. They promised to send us a lady the next day. That night we prepared for her. We hadn't a clue about hiring help. Should we leave her some lunch? We agreed to leave a can of soup, then discovered we had none. Carmella volunteered to go to the corner grocer and get a can, as well as a loaf of bread, some cheese and a carton of eggs. We never had more than a carton of milk or a few cans of beer in our fridge. After the shopping, we had just sat down to watch some TV when Carmella decided that the worker would most likely be from the Caribbean and shouldn't we get her some chicken, rice, flour?

"What do you think? Wouldn't she prefer that? Some solid food instead of these eggs and bread and canned soup?" I went out for provisions at a shop close by. By then we were out quite a few dollars.

When I got back from the shop I suggested to Carmella that we sort through the laundry. "Shouldn't we remove our personal articles?"

"What do you mean?" she asked.

"Well, like our panties and bras."

"For Christ's sake, don't you think the woman knows panties and bras?"

"Yes," I said, "but shouldn't we do those things ourselves?"

"Come on, girl. Then why are we hiring her? Why don't we just do it ourselves? For Christ's sake, she's not washing them by hand."

I was not convinced leaving all the laundry was the right thing, but I agreed with Carmella anyway. Then I made yet another trip to the shop. We had detergent but no fabric softener for the dryer. We did not use it but had seen it on many a TV commercial.

By then we were both tired and disgruntled. We sat in front of the TV, Carmella switching from channel to channel.

"I think we should take out some of the garbage from the kitchen," I said. "Especially the smelly bag of spoilt veggies; it's been there a few days."

"Why are we paying out good money to this woman?" Carmella asked in a flat voice. "What will there be for her to do? Do you think white folks do all of this?"

"But we're not white folks," I answered. Tired, I said goodnight and headed for the privacy of my room.

Early the next morning we were leaving for work when Carmella said, "You know, you're right. Let's take the bag out. Christ, it stinks."

"Why don't we leave a note for her along with the key?"

Dear Help. We crossed out, erased, changed the note several times. Finally we decided on:

Dear sister,

Welcome. Help yourself to food. Make yourself at

home. The cleaning items are in the kitchen cupboard.
The laundromat is two blocks away.

Thank you in advance.

Sister to sister. Carmella was the first to get home that evening. I found her in the living room, in front of the TV with a scotch in her hand. "What's the celebration?" I joked. "Isn't it too early for that kind of drink?"

"Look." She pointed to the four garbage bags in the middle of the room. "Feel the inside, the clothes are wet. What did she do with all those quarters? And you would think she could at least have folded them, or put them out to dry on the radiator."

Our dirty dishes were still stacked in the sink. The food untouched. The bathroom half-clean.

"God, even I could have done a better job in my sleep."

I poured myself a drink and sat down beside Carmella.

"Look, maybe it isn't her fault," I volunteered. "Maybe the agency didn't tell her that she was coming to an apartment, and one without laundry facilities. Maybe she took it for granted that she was coming to a home with its own washer and dryer where at least she could put her feet up and watch television while the clothes washed."

"So what are you saying?" Carmella asked with more than a touch of irritation. "That working-class people can't have help? Didn't we pay for the help with our hard-earned money?"

"I'm not defending her," I said, realizing I should have kept quiet. But it was too late, so I continued. "Maybe she resented walking the two blocks to the laundromat with the four garbage bags. I'm sure cleaning ladies have their standards, you know."

"But she didn't even eat our food," Carmella added in a bewildered voice.

"Well, maybe she didn't want to do us out. Maybe she's used to a couple cans each of things in cupboards, not one can of soup, one can of corned beef, one loaf of bread. Maybe she's used to a freezer full of stuff in the basement. Maybe she was just being kind to us."

The next month, we pushed our dirty laundry to the laundromat, bought a Saturday paper and read while the clothes washed and dried.

"You know something, I don't blame the woman. This is boring shit, and there isn't even a television," said Carmella. We both broke up in laughter.

After the cleaning woman adventure, I tried to busy myself, so as not to become involved in any more of Carmella's ideas. It didn't work.

———————

I unfolded the letter once again and read.

 Dearest, dearest friend,
   I miss you. It's not the same without you.

How could it be? I thought. I was always there, no matter how much I protested. The double date stands out. Carmella had come in giddy from her poetry class one evening. That was when I gathered that she had found a guy she really liked, apparently a fellow poet.

"Have you ever been on a double date?" she asked me casually one night.

"No," I answered, not paying enough attention.

"Well, how about a double date?" she asked, quite excited and nearly out of character. It should have been a warning, but I didn't hear it as such.

"Sure," I said.

"Okay, then we have a double date two weeks from today. Leave everything to me."

"Wait a minute, who's my date?"

"Johnny's cousin. You'll like him; he's a handyman and he's cute."

I didn't trust her idea of cute, but I figured what the heck. Nothing much to lose. A meal at a restaurant, a movie or party. If I didn't like him, I wouldn't have to go out with him again. Then Carmella told me we would be going on a picnic in the afternoon, an hour outside the city, and after that, horseback riding. I almost choked on the cracker I was eating.

"What? Horses? Wait a minute, Carmella. The closest I ever got to anything resembling those beasts was a donkey. No way."

"I can't believe you. Where's your sense of adventure? Please. Come on, girl."

"Okay, Carmella. But if I fall off and die, you're responsible."

Looking back, I swear Carmella should have been an actress, but I guess poets have to be good at drama.

I slept badly the night before the date. The next day was lovely. The weather was hot with a soft breeze blowing. My date turned out to be gentle and good-mannered. We had lunch. We lounged on the grass. Played a game of volleyball and drove off to the horses. I confessed to my date that I had never been on a horse. "Don't worry," he said. "They're gentle creatures. They won't hurt you."

We were on the road for another hour. Carmella was navigating from the back seat.

We reached our destination. A row of horses was lined up waiting for us, their tails switching flies away. Another dozen people were waiting to saddle up. The stablehands put us in groups of four. We were the only non-whites.

It was awkward getting onto the horse. Three times I swung my leg up but couldn't make it. Finally, one stablehand had me step into his hands and a second boosted me over. I sat stiffly in the saddle. Carmella rode ahead with her date. My date and I were in the last group. We came to a small creek, and the horses drank water and moved on. Mine did not move on. It stood there drinking and would not follow the rest.

My date stayed behind to help. "Use your foot on it. Teach it who's boss."

I did this timidly. The horse still didn't move. I didn't want to be too rough, afraid he would throw me off.

I didn't hear the description of the land, the history of the area. My full attention was focussed on the beautiful creature that so terrified me. The warm afternoon passed slowly as I held onto the reins. My date was close by, but that was cold comfort.

When we arrived back at the stable I jumped off quickly, falling to the ground, hurting my legs, but it was worth it.

"Great!" said Carmella behind me. "Let's do this again soon." My date winked at me.

We got home just in time for the TV sports. Carmella was very happy. "Winter is coming," she announced. "Let's go skiing, I know a place . . . "

I had stopped listening, images of the horse still in front of me.

Without warning, Carmella got up one day and decided that she was moving out to Yellowknife. "The sun shines all night," she said. "Let's move out there."

I declined, promising to visit. Carmella begged but I was determined. Carmella moved on, and I never visited. I got married. Had babies. And treasured my friendship with Carmella.

I really did miss her. I remembered writing her to tell her I was getting married and asking her to be my maid of honour. She refused, telling me why in a letter. Thinking of that letter now I retrieved it from the pile and smoothed out the creases.

Got your letter. I hope you know what you are doing. As you must know, I don't agree with this marriage thing. It seems to me the question of autonomy is not negotiable in marriage. We will disagree for some time on this, but you know me: I do not believe that friends have to agree on everything. Of course, you will not take my advice, you'll plunge in.

Enough! For God's sake, girl, write soon.

Love, C.

Her letters kept me alive. I lived through them. They provided that glimmer, that spark during periods in my life when night takes over and the dawn becomes a memory. I looked down again at her latest letter and read the note scrawled at the bottom:

P.S. P.E.I. will be great. Come out and visit. Have you learned to swim yet? I bet not. Come let me teach you next summer.

Yes, I thought to myself, maybe next year.

THE TRAVELLING MAN

He was always a mystery man to us. We had no memory of him. Mother never talked much about him. Dim memories like rain-soaked photographs blow back and forth in my mind. I'm lying in bed, half awake. I'm in that place where I was born but never knew because Mother took us away before we could walk. I never smelled the soil. I don't remember the stars.

There was the knowledge that I would grow up and leave the place my dream takes me back to. Water on both sides, trees and weeds growing wild, a gully with its insides rotting.

I wasn't the only one who knew. It was a legacy old as time. Everyone left. Some went back, but they all left. In the dream, sometimes there is a ship, but usually there is a plane. In the dream, it soars over the ocean, over winter-frozen water. Me, my brother and mother soaring. Bird. Free. Plane. Another land.

I'm split. I'm two persons: one the little girl, standing with blue-green water on each side; one the woman in the cold. Frozen bones. I'm a child struggling to wake from a nightmare. I'm a woman looking for lost bones, searching. I knew that we would leave the land, travel, come to this place, and that I would be an old woman. Frozen, broken bones. But now I'm the little girl again.

We left without telling Father. I couldn't talk. I couldn't walk. Big Brother and Mother leading the way. Big Brother knew something of father, that he was a travelling musician, moved from town to town. When he came home he slept, strummed his guitar. Big Brother says the music from the guitar was of a far-off land.

I tried to dream the land but couldn't, for I didn't know it, its language or rhythm.

This mystery man. This travelling musician. This dancing chameleon. I wish I could hold on to him, look at him, feel him, smell him, touch him, perhaps kiss him, let him hold me. I hear the strumming of his guitar and his voice calling out to a land far, far away, one with another language, with the beat of drums.

Cold here, but it is home. Frozen lake, I don't have to dream it. No smell of Father's home.

I ask Mother to tell me about Father. "He is a musician," is all she says. What was he like? "Here's a photo." She throws it carelessly at me. It's a Polaroid of a man holding a guitar. I stick the picture on the bathroom mirror and stare into the mirror. "Mama, people say I look like him. Mama, do I look like him?"

"You look like yourself," she says softly.

People tell me and Big Brother that our hands are like his. Mother gets mad.

"Your hands are like your hands," she sighs.

People say we can play music like him, that the rhythm is in our blood and our hands.

"It is my hard-earned money that pays for your music lessons that make you sound so good," Mama points out.

It's confusing. This travelling musician, Mother doesn't say much about him. Sometimes I wish she would just curse him. That way I would get to know things about him: what he eats, doesn't eat, how he laughs, what he likes to wear, things like that. Mother won't talk. She just won't talk about him.

That doesn't seem to bother Big Brother. He says that when he grows big and goes away from Mother, he will play music just like Father, join a band and visit the land of travelling musicians.

I want to see the mystery man too. But I want Mother to go with me, to hold my hand when I look at him, to steady me when I step onto the land and when I hear the wave of the sea and smell the heat of the land.

I'm lying in bed, trying to get up. It's Father's Day.

"Mother, tell me about Father."

"What's there to tell? He's a travelling musician."

"Tell me more, Mother."

"Look at the photographs. They can tell you lots more."

I search through my box of old photos and see his face, his hands and his guitar.

"Look harder," Mother says. "The pictures can tell more than I ever could."

I search the faded old photographs. I see Mother looking at the travelling musician. She is young, a girl in a short cotton dress holding a baby, a little boy hanging on to her dress. The man has one arm around her, the other holds his guitar. He smiles at the camera. I look hard at the photographs, to know Mother, to know the travelling man.

OLD HABITS DIE HARD

Old man, skin scaly tree bark to touch. Rust eyes, water hazy. The iron is gone. Legs, arms, ready kindling. Bedbug. Bedridden. Bedlam. Bedpan. Bedraggled. Bedfast.

Faeces don't give ear to him any more. Old man in diapers. Old man in white gown. Mashed potatoes with milk is all he can eat. Old man needs steady hand to feed him. Out of habit, old woman folds clean, neatly ironed pajamas. Clean towel. Wash rag. Enamel carrier filled with mashed potatoes.

Disordered eyes. Looks past visitors. Old man recollects just one, old woman. The others bear no memory. Disappointed, you can see it on their faces, the tight turn of the lips, the begging in the eyes. Talk to us. Touch us. Remember us. He only sits, no teeth to his grin. Old man looks and looks. Memory escapes. No longer father, husband, grandfather, uncle, brother, friend.

Old man pulls towards old woman. Grab him, he'll shit, piss on the floors, run around like a madman, a bedlamite. The visitors approve of the restraint. We love him, they say. Old man wants to run, old man wants to go home. The visitors go. Room too depressing: some stringy flowers in a mug, a plastic balloon the only grace, a heavy curtain shuts out the light.

Old woman stays behind. She feeds him potatoes, eggs, milk through a straw. She talks to him. He cannot answer. She tells him things, answers for him. His hands are cool. She pulls the blankets closer to his body. His face sweet like dark plums. Time to leave. Keepers in white come to lead her out. She kisses old man. Water in his eyes. He stares. He stares. Night is a black sheet. Old man pass away, old man dead, old man gone. She had felt it. Hands cool, getting cold, heat leaving the face, purple turning black, eyes turning.

The mourners come, eat, sing, cry, drink, help to bury him. They go home. Old woman must bury him a second time: clothes to give away—Salvation Army, Goodwill; mattress to turn over; bank account to settle; pension to straighten out. One pot to cook, one mouth to feed. Out of habit, old woman does the wash, folds her nightgown. She always irons it. Washes towels, washes rags, folds them. Those go into the suitcase. Changes her bed sheets. Best pillowcase; lovely lace, that. Lies down. Pulls up the black sheet of night.

BLUE BELLE

———————————

I

She was a heavy drinker. Those who lived in the immediate neighbourhood knew this. Some said she first started drinking an occasional baby cham. Now, she was known as a confirmed rum drinker and an alcoholic.

She wasn't one of those who needed a drink every day. Three, four months would pass without a drop of alcohol to her mouth. Then, without warning, she would take up residence in the local rum shop. To outsiders, her binges looked unplanned and out of rhythm. They came once every three months and lasted three weeks. At the beginning of that month, the postman would bring a registered letter with an enclosed money order, postmarked Toronto, Canada. After she put away for the light bill, gas, water, and a little in the bank, the binge began.

She began drinking in the cool hours of the tropical morning, and continued through the harsh midday sun and then its replacement by the moon. It was not unusual for her to pass out in the rum shop, to be lifted onto two adjoining chairs to sleep it off. By the end of the second week, her lips were cracked, blistered as if burned by a hot iron. Her strong, tight face puffed up like a battered overripe breadfruit. Her skin dried to the colour of ash from a lack of care and wash. When she was not too drunk to walk, she staggered home. Some evenings when her body could take no more alcohol, her drinking companions supported her to her yard.

Through it all she never gained a bad reputation, remaining Blue Belle to her contemporaries and Miss Blue to the younger folks. They loved and accepted her, unlike her family, which was always in a state of anxiety about her activities.

Her sister, Rose, was forty, married with three children, and ran a grocery shop with her husband. She was deeply disturbed by Blue's life. "Ah don't know, ah just don't know why she haffi go on like dis and embarrass we so." Her husband pretended not to hear. "Yuh don't care, do yuh?" she snapped at him. His face was tense. He did not care, at least not like Rose did. He was bored with her criticism of Blue Belle.

"Ah care, yuh know. Ah care, but Blue is a big woman. Weh yuh expect mi fi do? When yuh not criticizing her drinking, it's her son yuh criticize. Concentrate on our life, is not like our life perfect!" he said with finality, going inside the house to pour himself a drink. Disappointed with his response, Rose called across the fence to her long-time friend. "Babsy, Babs!" she shouted, skillfully climbing over the barbed-wire fence.

Seated on the cool verandah with a glass of lemonade, she complained to her friend, "Ah don't know weh is wrong wid dat woman. She have notten to worry about. She have five grown children, four in foreign sending her money every month. She got a house, a nice flower garden and her own business. What else she want to be happy?"

She did not really expect an answer. This was not the first

time she had sat complaining to Babsy. Her voice trailed off into tiredness. Her friend offered her another glass of lemonade, but she waved it away. "Ah just don't understand, Mama and Papa never drink. Papa never even had a beer or anyting like dat, even on special occasions." She paused, then continued, "And Grand-mammy and Pappy never drink. I don't drink, our two older brothers, Barry and Junior, have only di occasional beer." She paused again and shook her head in disbelief. "And now to have a sister who is a rum drinker, and worse, a drunkard. . . . "

She was getting emotional, her eyes brimming with tears. She cared about her sister, but only insofar as Blue Belle interfered with her own church activities and reputation in the small community. Her, a committed church sister, Blue Belle, the community drunk, and Blue Belle's son, Jesse, an altogether different story.

II

Blue Belle was a woman of substance, above average height with broad hips and large breasts. Her face was handsome, bold, not a line, not a crease, not a crack in it, younger looking than her fifty-one years. Her black hair, cropped short, had a tiny white patch at her right temple, the size of a dollar coin. When sober, she was a model to any church or school activity.

Blue Belle had had her first child at fifteen years, her last at thirty. Two daughters and two sons lived abroad, and Jesse, her youngest, lived with her. She had never married, but not for want of suitors. In her youth she was known as the village Belle.

She was not a woman who talked a lot about herself. The only time she opened up was in the rum shop.

"All a dem come out good. Come, mek mi knock wood as ah still have one to see through. But all di others abroad wid big, big job. One a mi daughter dem is an accountant, di odder one is a nursery school teacher. Den mi big son, him is a assistant bank manager and di second son, him a study law."

When she told this story, the rum shop would grow quiet. Sentimental tears would roll down Blue's puffy face.

"Me alone raise dem. Me one feed dem, clothe and school dem. Not a man deh round." Wiping away tears, she would continue, the bar quiet except for the occasional sucking sound of lips on beer bottles.

"Me alone, me one," Blue would drone on. "Tek care a dem, not a penny from a man, not a dime. Is mi perseverance and mi goodness to odder people pickney mek di Lawd God help me fi send dem go a foreign so dem can come to someting."

"Ah remember when I use to take in wash to pay di children school fees and sew school uniforms for all di pickney dem inna di neighbourhood. For a while I was even a barmaid. Dem days, every bwoy after me for I did look good. Mi body fit, fit! Lawd, mi seh mi never have money fi buy di latest clothes, but when mi set out to sew miself a outfit, it mek dem frock inna di shop window dem look like a joke."

Blue paused to drink.

"Is when I was working as a barmaid mi meet Jesse father. Di man did want to married, but mi never inna di marriage business and mi never know how him would treat mi odder pickney dem. So, mi seh to miself, see yah Blue, no bodder tek up any crosses pon youself what you cyaan deal wid little more down di road. Better you jus mek dat sacrifice fi you odder children first. Next ting you know, man come waan rule you and dem! Is a whole heap a hard times mi go tru to give dem what fi mi parents couldn't gi me."

Then, her mood would change from nostalgia to "Round of drinks on me. Mek we drink to good friends and Jamdown best products!"

Some days the older rum shop patrons debated Blue Belle, casting bets as to when she first started drinking. Did it coincide with the desertion of her last love or was there some other reason they did not know? They never came to any particular conclusion.

Blue Belle lived quite comfortably in a lower-middle-class neighbourhood. She rented out her house for weddings and special functions. She also sewed wedding gowns and supplied flowers from her garden. Her youngest son shared the three-bedroom house with her.

III

Jesse made his living as a chef in a large, affluent hotel. By all standards he was a good son, though his effeminate nature worried Blue. She feared for his safety in certain areas of the city where there was a belief that men like Jesse should be stoned to death. She cautioned him that his laughter was too much like a woman's. He was her favourite child. She spoke often to her friends about him. "Yuh know, ah love dem all, di four abroad, but Jesse is my boy. Him is like a son and daughter all in one."

"Him help mi good wid di floral arrangements dem and di planning of di weddings. And don't talk about how him can cook."

One would not describe Jesse as a handsome man. He was pretty, his face had fine bones, a delicately drawn mouth, with skin soft and dark like evening dusk. His hair was cropped close to his head and had the identical white patch as Blue's, and his hands were expressive, with long, slender fingers.

Jesse fussed over Blue Belle, bought her clothes, often accompanied her to a movie or a bingo game. She, in turn, would follow him to cricket matches or to the pantomime. He called her Mums. He travelled frequently to Florida and New York to visit friends, often bringing back material to make her new dresses, perfumes, canned goods and other items hard to get on the island. Jesse invited friends from abroad to visit. He entertained lavishly with good food, drink and music. Some of his friends returned to the island many times. Others came only on one trip.

They were all friendly men and women, easy and relaxed. Blue Belle liked that about them.

Her favourite, though, was Peter. A regular visitor to the house, she had first met him years ago when Jesse brought him home from New York. He was close to Jesse's age, in his mid-twenties. He was short, neither slim nor fat. He had a thick waist, a boyish grin and bright grey eyes. He treated her respectfully and with genuine warmth and affection. He had many women friends and talked about his mother and sisters constantly. She liked that. He gave Blue gifts and made much of her beautiful garden. On one of his many visits, Peter asked Blue if he could call her Mums.

"Yuh can call me Mums as soon as Jesse tek yuh down to di beach and put some colour on dat pale skin," she bantered.

Peter was good at playing cards, dominoes and Ludo. His smile was quick and open like her son's. She secretly hoped they would remain friends and that Jesse's trips to New York would be more frequent. She could not forget, try as she did, that night three years ago when he was badly beaten up by a pack of men and had to be hospitalized.

"Hey, faggot bwoy!" they taunted. They hurled stones at Jesse. He tried to run, but was no match for them. They felled him with kicks to his body and face and pelted him with stones.

"Batty bwoy, bulla. We come fi run you out. We don't want no batty bwoy roun yah." Their chants took on a religious fervour. "Pussy, we come fi kill you, yuh little blood claat. Dis is a warning."

They ran off when an approaching car stopped, shining its lights on them. The passengers were friends of Blue's. Blue was not a church-going woman, but that night she prayed that God would guide Jesse to America soon.

She put word out that there was a little money offered to anyone with news about the men who beat Jesse. It was a futile attempt, but she did find out that they did not live in the area, so she rested easier.

Their lives resumed. Jesse continued his job as a chef. During his holidays he travelled to New York and Florida, his friends visited and Blue Belle had her binges. Rose kept interfering in her sister's life. She thought of Jesse and sucked her teeth. "As to him, him is just another lost cause. Him so devoted to Blue that him blind. Everyting seem normal, di binges and himself." She sucked her teeth again, muttering, "Lord, show me a sign. Will you sweep away di righteous wid di wicked? Have mercy on yuh good shepherds. We doing yuh work di best we can."

IV

Except for Rose's church sisters, no one objected to Blue's household. The community was small and people loyal. People seldom moved and some lived for years in the same house. Houses were scarce and rents high in the city, so many people added an extra room onto their house, to accommodate relatives moving from the rural areas to join friends and family in the city.

Virgil was one such fellow who moved into the community to live with his aunt and uncle and their children. Short and slim, Virgil was all bones without fat, somewhat like an underfed dog. He had a small head with eyes the colour of slate. Virgil was a shade or two lighter than Jesse, and though not a handsome man, he exuded a certain forceful energy that attracted people to him. He was in his early twenties, seemingly forthright and friendly.

Virgil assisted his uncle, who owned a small shoemaker's shop, repairing and re-building shoes. Though he worked hard and long, this was not Virgil's idea of a career and it did not match his dreams of living in the big city. In the village where he came come from, he had heard he could get rich quick, but so far he was having no luck. He sometimes visited nightclubs, but he was spending too much money, more than he could afford. He was not a rum shop person and found no recreation in listening to stories told by the regulars.

His evenings were spent hanging out at the front gate of his uncle's yard, watching people go by. Some evenings he played cards with guys next door. He was a good player and when they gambled for money he often won. But he was not interested in their company. They were content playing cards all day, eating, drinking, never moving from where they sat. He was not content. He wanted to make money, buy expensive clothes, own a car, maybe a house, have children. He was curious about Blue Belle and her son Jesse and had witnessed two or three of Blue's binges since he had moved into his uncle's house. He watched Jesse and Blue Belle, coming down the road, arm in arm, Jesse balancing and guiding his mother, children trailing behind them.

He asked around, but did not find out much. Blue Belle had children abroad, she was born in the community, her son was a chef, Blue Belle liked the rum shop, children and adults loved and respected her. Virgil saw Jesse several nights coming from work.

"Howdy sah, how yuh doin tonight?" Jesse waved at him, slowed down and walked towards the fence.

"Ah, sah, could be better. Ah tired, Friday and Saturday nights very busy, and some of dem high-brow people too demanding. Dem want yuh to cook and create all kinds of dishes dat dem taste one or two time in a foreign restaurant or weh dem see on TV. Dem cyaan remember di name of di dish, yet dem want you to mek it from dem description."

This comment had Virgil laughing loudly in delight, his skinny frame bent up like a worm passing through a baby's behind. "Tell me more bout dis workplace. It sound like nuff jokes," Virgil encouraged, leaning closer over the fence. They talked for a long time into the night. That marked the beginning of a friendship between the two men. Jesse stopped off at the gate most nights to talk. He told Blue Belle about Virgil and she suggested that he invite him to dinner.

Blue welcomed Virgil warmly but cautiously. He was excited and in a high mood and won her over by the end of the evening.

He surprised both mother and son with his capacity to eat like a rooting pig, cleaning out every last scrap on his plate, washing it down with a tall glass of sweet drink. He talked late into the night about his ambitions and dreams, engaging both Blue and Jesse with his enthusiasm.

Despite her cautiousness, Blue was taken with Virgil. She liked ambitious people and was impressed with all the things he wanted to do. She believed in hard work and was proud of her own achievements. "Yes son, dat is how I like to hear young people talk. If I can help at all, mek mi know."

Blue was a kind-hearted woman, often helping people, either by solving problems or lending them money. She was, however, not a foolish woman and prided herself on being an excellent judge of character.

Virgil became a familiar face in Blue Belle's house. He helped around the yard, doing jobs for her, climbing the coconut tree, picking fruits, cutting the grass, pulling weeds from the garden, riding his bicycle to pick up grocery items and delivering flowers.

v

The first time Jesse visited Virgil's yard he was not prepared for the sight hidden behind the high white-washed fence and sweet-scented flowering trees. A small dilapidated house with pieces of cardboard tacked onto broken window panes, some falling apart where the rain had beaten too much against them. Inside, the house was dark and airless. There were two rooms; one held a double bed, two single beds and a mat with sheets and pillows thrown on the floor. The other room served for cooking, eating and as the social area. It had an old sofa against the wall and a small table next to a kerosene stove. Virgil slept in a small area off of this room, partitioned by washed-out flour bags. Jesse and Virgil sat there on Virgil's single bed to escape the commotion outside. It was like traffic dead-ended on a one-way street.

"Jesse, ah need to better myself, man, because ah have ambition and work hard." Virgil talked in a quiet voice, lowering it even more. "Ah need to get out of 'ere, dis place is too stiflin'," he ended in an empty voice. Jesse could only put his arm around Virgil's shoulders to comfort him.

"Ah just need a chance, dat's all. Ah can't reach anywhere workin' and livin' 'ere," he said, quietly pointing to the back of the yard where the shoe shop was housed. He was looking into Jesse's face, pouting like a little boy.

He moved closer to Jesse and rested his head lightly on his shoulder.

"Bwoy, yuh don't know how lucky yuh is. Ah wish ah had a mother like Blue." Jesse squeezed his hand in answer. Behind their screen of flour bags, it was crowded and hot. There were no windows and the noise coming from the television set in the next room, a radio nearby and children's voices was deafening. Sensing Jesse's discomfort, Virgil, putting his finger in his mouth, jokingly said, "And Jesse, ah wish yuh was mi big brother, yuh could teach me whole 'eap. And mi is a quick learner." He paused and realizing Jesse's mood had not changed, quickly added, "Jesse, yuh could teach me how to cook, maybe ah could get a job in a restaurant." This made Jesse laugh.

"Bwoy, yuh tink servin' people food easy? Tek mi advice, try another profession." He was again at ease, gesticulating as he talked. Virgil liked him in this mood.

"But still, it can't be as hard as shoemakin'. Yuh ever in a situation weh a man give yuh instructions to mek shoes, 'im draw it on di paper, everyting, and den when yuh hand 'im di shoes, 'im seh is di wrong size and wrong colour?"

They were curled up on the bed, like two rude schoolboys trading jokes. Virgil told Jesse about his brief apprenticeship as a waiter before he moved to the city. "Ah did always feel like di cooks get di best of both worlds—dem can even eat before di customers."

"But, what about when complaints come back to di chef? When dem haffi do over a whole meal, because somebody find hair or fingerprint on di plate?"

"Fingerprint? Come, man, come wid someting else." Virgil challenged him, their laughter and talk competing with the fuss outside.

"Yes, fingerprint, mi nah joke. Yuh nuh understand. How long yuh stayed as a waiter?"

Virgil confessed that he had only lasted for a month. He did not say why he left. They continued their joking, each trying to outdo the other.

Two days later Virgil left to visit his sick mother. They did not see each other for weeks.

VI

Virgil's mother died leaving nine children behind. Virgil was the youngest. When he came back to town, he spent more and more time in Blue's yard. He began to call her Mums.

One night in Jesse's room, he suggested that he move in. "Ah could help more, be a real son and brother."

Jesse agreed. "Yes, mek me talk to Mums tomorrow."

Blue was pleased. Virgil had come to be like another son. She secretly hoped that he would influence Jesse in more "manly" ways. She gave her blessing.

The move was not complicated: one pair of shoes, three pairs of pants, two shirts, three T-shirts, half a dozen pairs of underpants, a toothbrush, a washcloth and a towel.

He kept on working for his uncle, returning to Blue and Jesse in the evenings, becoming an established member of the household. Virgil took his turn bringing Blue home from the rum shop. The community began to see him as Blue's other son. They became a trio. During Blue's sobriety they went on outings and made plans, and conducted their domestic affairs like a family. Virgil and Jesse spent a lot of time together, epecially in the quiet of the late evening, when work was done, pots and plates washed, and the chickens asleep in the coop.

Jesse was growing tired of his job, the long hours, the meagre wage and no promotion. Virgil, too, complained vigorously about wasting his talent on poor people's old, stinking shoes, about not having enough money. Later they talked with Blue Belle about their plan to go into business together.

Virgil started out: "Mums, yuh know we always complaining bout all work and little money." He paused a bit, uncertain, looking to Blue for encouragement. She nodded.

"Well, Jesse and me tinking dat we could start up a shoe business and be our own boss."

Blue listened while Virgil did most of the talking.

"So, Jesse, weh yuh have to say?"

"Well, Mums, ah agree because ah tired of di hackling in dis job." She listened while they continued talking about their plans. They would buy leather for the shoes. Jesse would keep his job for a while and Virgil would leave his uncle's employment. He would learn to drive a car, and later they would investigate equipment for making shoes, eventually finding one or two men to work for them. Virgil would sell the shoes at the market and on the sidewalk in front of the big department stores.

"Ah give unnu mi full support," Blue enthused. The following day she went to the bank and withdrew money to help them put their plans into action.

VII

The first driving school instructor came in a small, rusty, fifteen-year-old car to pick up his pupil. Onlookers teased and laughed at the car, but the instructor, bursting with confidence, assured Blue and Virgil that he had taught many students in the same car and they had all passed their driving test in record time. "Yu see dis car? Is a good luck buggy dis," he declared. "Is good luck wah mek me nuh trade it in and buy a new one." Though he convinced Blue, Virgil and Jesse, the sidewalk spectators were not convinced. One young man heckled, "Is what model car dat? It look like a future model." The instructor was used to being teased and was in good humour when he drove off with Virgil, suggesting they begin their class on a quiet street in the suburbs. They did not return until way past dark. The car had overheated and shut off so many times that they could not start the lessons.

The instructor came again perhaps three times, until Blue told him not to come back. The second instructor arrived. The tires of his vehicle were as smooth as a bald man's head and of varying sizes. Hours later Virgil came back on foot. The car had turned over on its side while going down a steep and winding country road. Virgil came home with a bloodied knee, his pants ripped, his elbow and face bruised.

The third instructor arrived two days later, smelling of rum and tobacco. Jesse offered to ride in the back with them. When they got into the car, the new instructor promptly offered to sell Virgil a license. He would have bought it, were it not for Jesse's protest. A succession of instructors followed.

The final instructor came highly recommended by one of the regulars at the rum shop Blue frequented. He was a mature-looking man with a serious, no-nonsense face and a big belly riding over a thin leather belt. He took Virgil out twice a week and soon it was time to take the driving test. Virgil failed the first time, the second, the third and then the fourth. Virgil was fed up and so was Jesse. Blue called a conference with the instructor. They learned from him that the surest and fastest way to get a driver's license would be to buy it. The license was bought, and soon after a small van with enough room for shoes was purchased.

The three became closer. Jesse's flow of friends slowed. His foreign friends did not come as often. His friend Peter from New

York came a few times and then stopped. The last visit was fraught with tense quarrels between the two. Until Peter left, Virgil kept to the shoeshop they had built behind the house, and spent time with his uncle.

VIII

The business was going well and Jesse had left his job to work in the shop. Blue's binges continued. Virgil dreamed of a company where he was president, with a house of his own and children. He was also becoming tired of Blue, yet he could not leave. He was not independent enough and all the business assets were owned by Blue and Jesse.

He was tired of Blue's hold on Jesse. He had been a part of the household for over four years. He was confidant to both Blue and her son, and he knew he could manipulate Jesse. But Virgil also knew he had to be careful in his criticism of Blue Belle in his effort to swing Jesse over to his way of thinking. He thought of suggesting that they move out of the yard into a larger store, but he knew that Jesse would discuss it with Blue, who would probably see through the scheme. There was no apparent reason why they should move. They were doing well working out of the yard.

Virgil began to study Blue's binges and Jesse's reaction, waiting for the right moment, for he saw that Jesse was becoming increasingly agitated with his mother. The opportunity came during one of Blue's binges, when he found Jesse pacing restlessly, staring at the liquor cabinet and its empty bottles.

"Why she haffi drink out all of dis liquor? She don't drink vodka, she don't drink gin. Yet she drink out all mi liquor for guests." His voice was weary, with an edge of resentment. Virgil stayed quiet, comforting Jesse, squeezing his arm.

"Well, Jesse, ah don't want yuh to tink ah disrespect Mums, but ah tink yuh need to show her dat yuh tired of being a clean-up man." He paused, looking at Jesse for a reaction. Seeing that

Jesse was listening attentively, he went on, "Well, dis is what I would do. Don't buy back any liquor for di cabinet. Dis is weh yuh do all di time, right?" Jesse nodded.

"Well, ah tink yuh should full up all dose bottle wid pipe water, seal dem and put dem back in di cabinet. Dat's di only way yuh mek Mums know yuh mean business." Jesse looked uneasy.

"Ah don't mean to sound wicked and ungrateful," Virgil added quickly, "because you and Mums help me to really mek someting of miself, and both of you is family. Ah just as concern about her as you." Jesse made no move to respond, and Virgil, knowing Blue would be staggering in at any moment, pulled the bottles from the cabinet. He filled them with water and handed them to Jesse to return to the cabinet. Blue came home shortly after, led by two schoolboys from the yard next door, the back of her skirt covered in dog shit from a fall. Jesse thanked them, gave them a dollar and took Blue to her room, where she flopped back on the bed. He changed her clothes, cleaned her up and covered her with a light cotton sheet. Virgil had a cup of tea ready for Jesse when he came out. He gave Jesse a shoulder massage and they went to bed.

Late one night during the last week of Blue's binge she went to the cabinet for a drink. Virgil was the first to hear her. "Mums up. Ah bet she goin' to di liquor cabinet."

"Come mek we watch," said Virgil, excited. Jesse refused. He could not bring himself to see his mother so humiliated. Virgil got out of bed and quietly crept behind the sofa to watch. Blue reached for the vodka bottle. She poured the liquid into a glass and took a gulp. She looked at her glass in disbelief, then poured more, had another taste. She reached for another bottle, poured half a glass and sipped, her face a picture of confusion. Doubting her senses, she unscrewed the cap from the vodka bottle and drank straight from it. She became agitated and frightened.

Satisfied, Virgil shifted behind the couch, knocking a little figurine off a small table. He could not tell whether she had seen him. He moved quickly and disappeared. Maybe she would forget by tomorrow, he hoped, wishing he had a gallon of rum to soak her memory. He said nothing to Jesse.

Early the next morning Blue left for the rum shop. When she had not come back by evening, Jesse was worried. She had never gone out so early before, and never on a Sunday, which was the day she drank at home. He felt an empty ache in the pit of his stomach. Virgil persuaded him to go for a ride in the car. They packed a basket of food and headed for the beach.

Over fried fish and bread Virgil broached the idea that they move out on their own. "Jesse, yuh ever tink of having yuh own house?" he opened the subject.

"No, because it was always jus Mums and me. Never thought of it and weh mi was to get di money?" Virgil sifted sand through his fingers, thinking how to steer the conversation around to Jesse's bank account. He had spent most of his own money on fine things for himself. He sensed this was not the right time to pursue the conversation. They drove back home in silence.

Blue was not home when they arrived. Virgil was in no hurry to see her and left the house to visit his uncle. When she came home she went to bed. Virgil did not come home that night. He returned the next morning.

When Blue woke up, Jesse tried to talk to her. She only stared at him. He was uncomfortable and a little frightened. This was not the mother he knew. The strain in the house continued. Jesse and Virgil spent more time locked up in their room, with curtains drawn and windows closed.

One day when Virgil was out all day, Jesse tried again to talk with Blue. "Mums, what happen to us? Ah can't stand when yuh treat me like dis."

All Blue said was, "Ah have one advice to give yuh: be careful, careful of dat bwoy."

"Wah yuh mean? How? Wah Virgil haffi do wid me and you?"

"Ah have notten else to say, just be careful." She went outside to tend to her flowers. Worried and confused, but knowing he would not get another word out of her, Jesse left her alone.

The relationship between mother and son did not improve much. Blue felt the loss, but for the first time in her life was not sure of how to fight back. She had no one to confide in. She thought of her sister Rose, but quickly put the idea out of her head.

People in the community were unaware of the rift. Virgil acted the role of the perfect son in public and he continued to be polite and helpful to Blue. She found she was talking to herself often. Asking and answering her own questions, as to what went wrong. She concluded that there was something evil about Virgil. She cursed herself for not judging his character more wisely. What would he come with next, she wondered?

When Virgil suggested they buy the house that came up for sale across the street, Jesse was ready.

But Virgil cautioned, "Let we investigate it first, den tell Mums after. If we tell her before, ah know she goin' to try stop yuh. She don't want to see yuh independent."

Virgil was in charge of figuring out the financing of the house. Jesse agreed to front the money for the downpayment, but he needed Blue to sign the bank papers. Virgil tutored him on being firm when he talked to Blue, then disappeared for the night, insisting that it was better Jesse talk to his mother alone.

"Yuh know weh yuh doin', son?" Blue asked. "Yuh have a house here, yuh comfortable, nobody don't trouble yuh. So why because dis bwoy come into our life, yuh want to leave me and go buy a house to live outright wid him? Yuh no frighten? Yuh figat what dem do people like you?"

"Mums, is not like dat. We movin' the business over dere too, more space and ah still just across di street from yuh."

"Across the street from me? You mean right up in mi face for me to see your demise. Yuh tink a mother want to see dat? Ah don't tink is a good idea. In fact, is not a good idea. Son, ah can't mek yuh do it. Yuh is a idiot? Yuh don't read di paper, yuh don't read how dem killing all kind of big man who have more protection than you?"

"Mums, ah haffi do it. Ah want mi own place, ah want to be mi own man." She knew Virgil had put him up to this.

The mood was heavy. "Mums, I need your signature on the withdrawal paper for di bank."

She got up and dressed. They took the bus to the bank. Blue removed her name, releasing Jesse's savings solely to him.

"Mums, don't vex. Is something ah haffi do fi miself," Jesse pleaded.

"Ah only hope I don't live long enough to see yuh funeral," was Blue's reply. The conversation on the bus home ended.

On the day of Jesse and Virgil's move, Blue started on a binge. Slumped on a wicker chair on the verandah, she watched through watery eyes as her son and Virgil set up house across the street.

The binge ended, and life continued.

IX

Blue did not see Jesse often, sometimes a whole month passed with only a glimpse of him.

One night, Jesse appeared at her door. He had lost weight, his face was drawn and he had been crying.

Blue immediately fed him.

"Here eat dis, before yuh even start fi talk, ah don't like how yuh looking."

This was the story he told his mother:

"Mums, yuh know dat Virgil have baby mother? Yuh know all di time we living here with you, him have baby mother? All dem time when him say him at him uncle?"

Blue had suspected this a long time, but she did not say this to him. He did not need to hear that now, he needed her support and care. Most of all, understanding.

She let him talk.

"Mums, she come to di house last night. Cussing loud, say she have two pickney fi him, and dat he promise to let her move into him house. Him tell her me and him is just business partner."

Blue interrupted. "So weh Virgil was?"

"Him wasn't home. But I wait up for him. Him seh it was all a mistake, dat him wanted to tell me about it a long time ago, but him fraid." He paused for breath.

"Mums, him seh him not in love with her, that him love me. But she seh him come and see her every week."

"So what him seh, when yuh tell him dat?" Blue asked, holding on tight to the rage she felt building up in her heart.

"Him seh she lying. Him seh to prove dat he not in love wid her, he will give me di monthly allowance to send to di children."

Blue listened. She repressed the desire to curse Virgil. It was hard, but her concern for her son's welfare far outweighed her desire to say "I told you so."

"Well son, what yuh going to do?"

"Ah don't know, Mums. Mi don't waan lose him." He began to cry uncontrollably. She was repulsed by his weakness, his emotional dependence on Virgil. But he was her son, no matter what. She held him close and wiped his eyes. He was, after all, her flesh and blood. Jesse spent the night in his old room, but went home later the next day. He did not come back.

X

Business was good and Virgil was getting ready to open the first store, VJ's, downtown. For him, this was just the beginning. Virgil had plans to open stores all across the island. Over the years he had become stout, his face filled out, matched by a small paunch. His clothes were the best money could buy and his shoes were imported from Italy. By now he had several workers and a man in charge of driving the van. He owned a brand-new, four-door, dark blue car. But he was still discontent. Though Blue did not interfere in his affairs, he felt a loose string somewhere. She continued to have power over her son.

Having heard of an obeah man in the countryside, Virgil set off early one morning, on the pretense of checking out another location for a shoe shop. The dirt road which led to the obeah man's house was steep, curling with thick bush on one side, the sea on the other. It was a hard ride up; one wrong curve would send the car over. He was relieved when he finally arrived, grinding the car to a halt. Not a drinker, Virgil nevertheless took a shot of rum to settle his shaky nerves. The obeah man was expecting him. He was a powerfully built man, tall and muscular, his skin the colour of mud. Dressed in a long, flowing caftan made with a fabric in an African print and with a turban on his head, the man greeted Virgil. Virgil's contact had given him a rundown of the problem. He knew men like Virgil and had attended to similar problems. In other instances he had gotten rid of the lover's partner. He invited him to sit down, his voice gentle but forceful.

"What can dis man do for yuh, son?"

"Ah have a life and love problem," Virgil began, outlining his case. The obeah man's eyes never left Virgil's, and betrayed no surprise. Virgil found this unsettling, but it had the effect the obeah man wanted: fear, trust, larger-than-life power. He had practised obeah for over twenty years. The man asked Virgil a few questions about Blue and Jesse: their habits, their character, what they looked like, when they were born.

"So, yuh want me to use mi powers to let di boy love yuh more and him mother less?"

"No, ah want 'im to listen to me, become more dependent on me and lessen di mother power over 'im. Send her away if needs be. She have sons and daughters in foreign. Mek her go to dem and out of our life."

The obeah man did not like this sinister little man sitting across from him. But his job was to give his clients what they wanted, not to judge them.

"Dis will cost you. Is a difficult case, but not impossible."

"No problem, money not di problem. Di problem is Blue Belle."

Getting up and pulling down several sealed bottles from a cabinet, the obeah man set them on a table close by. He painstakingly measured powders, dried leaves and herbs from the bottles and wrapped them in brown paper. As he poured out portions of the powders onto paper, he never stopped talking.

"Yuh see all of dese tings? One need natural herbs, dis is di basic part of mi treatment. Herbs like cerassie, pepper, elder weed, jack-in-the-bush weed, guinea hen weed, sorrow weed, lion weed, bad fever weed, old woman weed, duppie battie weed, go-far weed. Ah tek all dese weed and a few other secret ingredients and dry some. Some ah juice and so on. Now ah goin' to give yuh dese herbs. Every chance yuh have, put dem into a drink or food dat dem eat. Burn dis incense every night. Dis paper 'ere, write di lady name on it. Put it in yuh shoes and walk on it. Go on a two-day fast. Don't even drink juice, only water. Wear dis oil at night in bed. Bathe wid dis before yuh go to bed."

Virgil took notes, sweat pouring from his face as his pen tried to keep up with the obeah man's instructions.

"Den yuh must seh dis three times a day: 'By St. Peter, by St. Paul, by di living God, ah want so-and-so brains and intellect not to overcome mine.'"

He continued, "Yuh do dat, follow everyting and ah will do mi job 'ere."

As the obeah man handed Virgil parcels of herbs and bottles of oil, he asked, "Di contact dat yuh use to come 'ere and see me, dem tell yuh dat ah don't work for local currency."

It was a statement rather than a question. Virgil had not been told, but it was too late to argue that point and he wanted Blue out of their lives.

"No problem, no problem." Pulling out his leather wallet,

Virgil counted out several large American bills for the obeah man. Despite his dislike for Virgil, the obeah man gave him a big smile, showing the perfect pink lining of his false teeth. It was good money for a few hours of work.

Virgil drove back to town, confident and happy. A few weeks after his visit to the obeah man and two days of walking on Blue's name she fell on the polished verandah tile and fractured her knee. She was taken to the hospital, where she spent two weeks. When she was released, Jesse took over her cooking and cleaning and kept her company.

XI

Confident that all was going well, Virgil encouraged Jesse to spend time with his mother. The day she came home from the hospital, he sent her a bunch of flowers with a card wishing her well, hoping they could forget the past and start over fresh. She accepted the flowers with a smile, not wanting to put up a wall between herself and her son. She knew how deep his feelings went.

That evening, Virgil washed and dressed in his brand-new Florida-bought shirt and pants. He stepped into his car, polished by some of the boys on the street, and drove off to visit his baby's mother. Jesse did not know about these visits. Virgil had told him it was over when he left Jesse in charge of sending the once-a-month cheque to the woman.

Virgil visited her as he pleased but offered her no extra money. Sometimes he bought her a new dress, a pair of shoes or some jewellery, pacifying her protests at his refusal to let her and the children live with him. He left her house early that night, explaining that he had a late business meeting with a client from Miami. He was actually late for a date with a schoolgirl whom he had promised a sales job in the shop. He was planning to take her out to dinner for an informal interview and then to a movie at the local drive-in cinema.

Blue was soon up and around, again looking after herself. When she sat on the verandah and looked across the street a certain sadness covered her face. She was glad that her son visited, but she could not control the fear and disappointment she felt for him.

"So wah yuh do in di business now, son?" she asked one evening while they were sitting in the back yard together.

"Well, mi supervise di factory workers and see everything runnin' okay. Virgil do di contact with stores, supervise di sales clerks, and travel."

"So yuh don't travel again? Ah remember yuh were a boy who like to travel."

"Mums, ah tired of di travelling and Virgil like to do dat. He like to go to Florida and meet all kind of people."

About to tell him again to be careful, she thought the better of it and changed the talk to his sisters and brothers abroad. She had heard stories about Virgil's carryings-on with women. A man friend of hers had told her some time ago that he had seen her adopted son and a young girl boarding the airplane for a weekend in Miami. The reports made her sick to her stomach but she had vowed not to interfere.

"Dis sore a fester too fast and mi have no cure for it, so better leave it alone. It done pass di water and Dettol stage," she mumbled to herself each time she heard a new story about Virgil.

Jesse often came in the evening to talk. Once he even confessed missing his old room, and the times they spent together, just the two of them. She was touched, but knew this was no longer possible.

"What is to be must be, mi son, and we can't bring back di past. Yuh haffi look at weh in front of yuh. Yuh happy?" He said yes.

She said nothing more and got up to cook her dinner. He offered to peel the yam and bananas, but she refused, joking that her hands needed the exercise. He felt like a stranger but did not know why. He walked out to the garden.

The lawn that had once been well-kept was now unruly with grass and weeds sprouting all over. Virgil had long since stopped looking after the yard, and since Blue had fractured her knee, it was not getting the attention it was accustomed to. There was an air of neglect about the house and yard. He could almost smell the decay.

XII

Virgil was frustrated. He made another trip to the obeah man.

"Dis time is bout di ole lady. Di man okay, but di mother still a shadow over me." The obeah man asked if there had been results. Virgil told him about the knee. "Dat is good but not enuff. She have to leave di place. Ah just won't be free until ah see di back of her, preferably on a iron bird, goin' any place. England, America or Canada, dem all di same to me. Ah just want her out of mi life."

The obeah man listened, then said in a slow drawn-out voice, "As ah seh before, notten is impossible, but weh yuh want mi to do now require di service of Delawrece. So ah will have to correspond with 'im and get some ointments by mail and do mi part from 'ere." He paused. "So ah don't have to tell yuh dat it goin' to cost yuh a little more dan di last time . . . due to postage and di long distance communication."

"No problem, boss," Virgil uttered in desperation. "Ah just want her to leave me in peace and ah will pay for dat peace."

The obeah man gave him another piece of parchment paper, told him this time to go on a four-day fast, to burn three red candles for two nights, and to bury some objects in Blue's garden.

"Yuh have to get some chicken blood, feathers, some broken rum bottles, a airline ticket, four dawg teeth, and a piece of clothing from di woman. Dig a hole and bury dem. Pour in di blood first. When yuh cover it wid di dirt, sprinkle it wid a bottle of white rum. Plant a hand of go-far weed di next day on di top."

Virgil thanked the obeah man, paid him and set off to town,

his mind already at work. The chicken feathers and blood would be easy to get. He would kill one of Mums' own fowl. Broken bottles, rum all were readily available. A piece of her clothing wouldn't be that difficult; he would pay some child to take it off the clothesline or do it himself at night. A used airline ticket he had in his possession from his last trip to Miami. The dog teeth would be the problem—he would have to figure that one out. He smiled at himself in the rearview mirror.

The skies were heavy with pockets of black clouds. Shifting gears, he pressed on the gas to race against the rainstorm. As he turned the corner onto his street, he spotted a dead dog lying in the middle of the road, its gut ripped open, fresh blood splattered on the asphalt, its eyes and mouth wide open. He slowed down the car and surveyed the carcass like a hungry John Crow.

Late that night in the heavy rain a local boy bent over the dead dog and with a sharp chisel removed four teeth from its mouth. For this he received two pairs of men's shoes and a pant length of cloth.

Early the next morning Virgil pulled a brassiere from Blue's line. That evening he told Jesse that he felt like having fried chicken for dinner. Virgil volunteered to kill the fowl and pluck it. Over dinner he told Jesse that he wanted to fix up Blue's garden and surprise her. He would do it, he said, very early the next morning.

He awoke at 4:30 a.m. and with a kerosene lamp set to work in Blue Belle's garden. By 10:00 a.m. every weed was out, the hedges cut, and the garden beds turned over and watered, with new flowers and plants. That night he planted the chicken blood, feathers, broken bottles, dog's teeth, airline ticket and brassiere behind the freshly trimmed bougainvillea.

XIII

Thirteen days later the postman brought an airmail letter from Blue's oldest daughter.

Dear Mama,

I'm longing to see you. I've won some money in a lottery—no, not that much. I'm still not a millionaire, didn't hit the jackpot. Enough, though, to treat you to a fantastic holiday. Your ticket will be coming registered in a few weeks.

Your loving daughter,
Blossom

P.S. You have two eager grandchildren waiting to meet their granny.

Blue folded the letter, placed it in its envelope and stuffed it into her brassiere. Before she left the island she went on one last binge.

Jesse was glad to see his mother go. Virgil's treatment of him was becoming embarrassing. He had discovered several love letters from women.

Blue was secretly excited too; this would be her first trip on an airplane. She had always wondered what Canada was like. Instead of peering at pictures of her grandchildren, she would meet them in the flesh. She was also eager to get away from the impending doom, if only for a little while. She had come to the realization that she could not save her son. He had prescribed his own destiny.

None was happier than Virgil. As the day approached, he made plans with the schoolgirl-turned-clerk to take her for a ride in the country and spend a night at a resort. He wished Blue an early goodbye and hurried off. Promising to be back on the evening of Blue's departure from the island, he explained to Jesse that this would give him time to spend with his mother.

Blue Belle packed and unpacked several times. Even with the help of Jesse and Rose, she was still undecided about what to take and how much. Never one to fuss over packing, this felt so final, though she knew the ticket was for a six-week stay. When the taxi came, Blue Belle and Jesse climbed in with the luggage. Rose and her husband followed in another car. Some of Blue's drinking buddies also drove out to the airport. Throughout the ride, Blue gazed out the window like an eager tourist. She held Jesse's hand all the way to the airport. She said her goodbyes with relief and sadness.

Jesse's aunt and uncle offered him a ride home, but he excused himself, saying he had an appointment. When they drove off, he flagged down a cab and headed home.

XIV

Virgil was expected soon. Jesse busied himself in the kitchen, preparing a special meal for Virgil: chicken, rice and peas, and a potato salad with a bottle of imported wine. Jesse heard the gate open and a car drive in. He automatically reached for two wine glasses and the corkscrew. The footsteps came up on to the verandah, paused and then the door opened. He was not prepared for a woman full with pregnancy, a young girl of four years at her side.

"Good evenin'. Ah come to see Virgil," she said while Jesse stared open-mouthed.

"Virgil not home yet, but he should come in soon," he said, now aware he was gaping. "Come in. Can ah offer yuh a soft drink, or a box juice?"

The woman refused, but the child accepted. They took a seat on the couch, where Jesse joined them. They sat in silence and waited.

MAKEDA SILVERA was born in Kingston, Jamaica, and spent her early years there before immigrating to Canada in 1967. Now living in Toronto, she is co-founder of Sister Vision: Black Women and Women of Colour Press, where she is the managing editor. Her previous publications include *Silenced*, an acclaimed collection of oral histories of Caribbean domestic workers in Canada; *Growing Up Black*, a resource guide for youth, and *Remembering G and other stories*, her first book of fiction. She is also the editor of *Piece of My Heart*, a ground-breaking anthology of writings by lesbians of colour.

STEPHANIE MARTIN is a Jamaican-born artist living in Toronto. She is the co-founder of Sister Vision: Black Women and Women of Colour Press. (She is a Sagittarius with Taurus ascendent and moon.)

PRESS GANG PUBLISHERS FEMINIST CO-OPERATIVE is committed to producing quality books with social and literary merit. We give priority to Canadian women's work and include writing by lesbians and by women from diverse cultural and class backgrounds. Our list features vital and provocative fiction, poetry and non-fiction.

A free catalogue is available from Press Gang Publishers, 101–225 East 17th Avenue, Vancouver, B.C. Canada V5V 1A6